THE PURPLE HEART

CHRISTIE A.C. GUCKER

Copyright © 2012, Christie A. C. Gucker

All rights reserved. No part of this publication may be reproduced, stored in a retrieval system, or transmitted in any form or by any means, electronic, mechanical, photocopying, recording, or otherwise, without the prior written permission of the publisher.

ISBN: 978-1-64713-908-7

Cypress, Texas

Edited by Toni Rakestraw
Cover by Chuck Baum

This book is dedicated to every man and woman who has served as a soldier to defend freedom for all. You are heroes. It is also dedicated to the families of those soldiers, who give up their fathers, mothers, husbands, wives, brothers, sisters, children and friends, so that we can have those freedoms.

Your sacrifices do not go unnoticed. Thank you all.

Special dedication to the soldiers in my family, my father John P. Choida, grandfather Stephen P. Gaida, brother-in-law Darren Dreher, and my grand uncles, who have served and continue to do so for our country.

CONTENTS

Prologue	1
1. Sydney	5
2. Aiden	13
3. Cheryl	28
4. Aiden	35
5. Cheryl	43
6. Aiden	50
7. Cheryl	60
8. Aiden	63
9. Cheryl	73
10. Aiden	77
11. Cheryl	81
12. Aiden	84
13. Sydney	90
14. Cheryl	93
15. Aiden	100
16. Sydney	103
17. Gina	110
18. Aiden	120
19. Cheryl	129
20. Aiden	132
21. Cheryl	141
22. Aiden	145
23. Cheryl	149
24. Aiden	155
25. Sydney	161
Acknowledgments	171
About the Author	173

PROLOGUE

When they brought him to me, I knew he wasn't going to make it through the night. I had the ominous feeling he wouldn't even make it through the next few hours. The damage to his body was well beyond anything that could be repaired. He seemed to be quite aware of it, too. My heart sank in my chest, as I would be the only one to help him now. I watched as everyone moved on to other soldiers and sat down beside him.

"My name is Sydney. Hang in there with me, okay? I'm going to stay with you. I'll be right here for whatever you need."

I held his hand in mine and stared into his eyes; they showed me how truly frightened he was. His hands were so cold, and growing increasingly colder. I tried to give him all my strength. It was all I could offer him.

"I'm dying, aren't I? I can't believe this is how my life ends. I don't want to die," he confessed in a shallow-breathed whisper. He was so young, probably only in his early twenties, with so much life yet to live ahead of him. Now he would never have that chance.

"There's nothing to be afraid of—I promise. It'll be beautiful on *the other side. I just know it. This life is only a stepping stone,"* I *tried to reassure him.*

"How do you know? How?" he pleaded softly, needing to hear my response.

I didn't have much of a response to offer him. I didn't know. To be honest, I was afraid to die, too. What if there really was nothing more after this life? Is this really how I chose to spend mine? In the grand scheme of the universe, each person's life is just a quick blip on the radar. It wasn't much time at all, if you thought about it that way. However, there was also a big part of me that wanted to believe there's something more *waiting for us after this little blip disappears.*

I'd love to come back, reincarnated into another person, to live every step of life. There were so many things I would love to do all over again, like being a baby in a father's comforting arms, having that very first kiss, or maybe falling in love. Falling in love; it was something I hadn't done yet in this life. Not true love, at least.

I wondered if I'd remember anything from my previous life. I believed some people might. Old souls, you know the ones I'm talking about. A child who says something so profound, you can only stand there dumbfounded, and be sure to spend too much time pondering it. I once heard a three-year-old say 'It's never too late for now.' I'd thought about that one for an entire month. In fact, I always would. I'd made it my life's mantra.

"I've held the hands of dying men before, too many of them. They've never looked frightened when they passed. They've always looked—at peace," I told him, as he squeezed my hand with what little strength he had left.

"It doesn't hurt anymore, you know? I can't feel the pain.... Wait. Wait. Is that my father? Yes, it is. I see my father. He's calling for me.... He's smiling. He's so young. I think I should go to him. I want to go to him."

"Then go to him. It's where you're supposed to be, that's why he's

here. He came for you. Don't be afraid. It's okay to go." Those would be the last words he would hear.

He smiled, and then his gaze shifted past me. He looked happy and at peace. Then he was gone. I felt my eyes well up with tears. No matter how many times I'd watched someone die, the emotions I felt were so strong. I never got used to it.

I waited until his hands went completely cold, while cradling them in my own. I covered his body with a white sheet, said a quick prayer for him, and left the room.

1

SYDNEY

When I woke up that morning, I felt like something was slightly off balance. I wasn't exactly sure why. After coming straight home from work the night before, I had only made myself dinner and watched a movie. Maybe I was forgetting something? I just couldn't put my finger on it so checking my planner to make sure would be one of the first things on my list. I got up slowly and caught a glimpse of myself in the mirror. My reflection looked healthy and refreshed, but I certainly didn't feel it. My long hair was matted to my head with sweat, making a faux turban. I ran my fingers through it to try to pry it loose. The nightmare had disrupted my sleep again. As hard as I tried, I just couldn't remember this one. I often didn't remember them at all, but knew this one was about the war. I could remember hearing gunfire and panic, but that was it. There had been a lot of similar dreams lately, and they felt more like recurring distant memories. I guessed it was a bit of my very own Post Traumatic Stress Disorder. There was no way you could enter war and not be affected by it somehow. Every soldier had some form.

I had been working with soldiers returning from war for about three years now. Some of their stories had repercussions on my vivid imagination. But I had my own stories, having originally been an army nurse during the war on the *front lines*; you could say. I had watched many of the soldiers in my care die from traumatic wounds. It was what I did when there was nothing we could do to save them. I helped them accept their fate the best I could in the short time we had, in order for them to move on in peace. These men didn't have to die if it weren't for the greed and selfishness of power-hungry tyrants. It all seemed so tragic and unnecessary. It proved to actuate my perspective on life, enough to bend my career in a different direction. I wanted to work with the living once my tour was up because I could no longer care for the dying. It was too final for me. I had considered becoming an OB nurse, helping to bring life into this world rather than watch it leave, but that just didn't feel right. I wasn't quite sure why. Instead, I returned to school and received my degree in Psychology, so that I could continue working with the military, but this time as a civilian. Now, I help the soldiers return to life outside of the military instead of guiding them to their end. I help them find their way again. I help them find their life.

I had just seen so much of their suffering, and I really wanted to help them when they returned home, maybe help myself a bit, too. These soldiers had seen and done so much more than I had. Some of them were so young. They needed my help to acclimate back into a peacetime world. They needed help to forget. I hoped it would help me forget also, but some things were just embedded too deep within our soul to be forgotten. So I helped in any way I could.

I headed downstairs to put a pot of coffee on; it'd be ready once I'd showered. My footsteps echoed as I climbed the stairs. This house was too big for me. I had inherited it from my parents. It wasn't a mansion by any means, just too much for one person. The house itself was beautiful though, and I loved it. It was a two story with cathedral ceilings and hardwood floors throughout. The entire house was very open and you could see every room from, well, every room. Even the second floor had a landing overlooking the bottom floor. I kind of liked that aspect of the house. I was nervous being alone all the time, and it was comforting to be able to see there was no one lurking in the corners. Even though I was in a development, my house sat back from all the others, in a secluded wooded area via a long gravel driveway. I had my privacy, but sometimes I longed for the company of my neighbors. I had no idea who any of them were by name. I never even saw them except when driving down the street, offering a casual but friendly wave out of simple politeness.

My house was warm and cozy, even though it had a ton of open space. My earth-tone couches were big and cushy, with patterned throw pillows galore. I had pictures of my parents and much of my childhood, scattered amongst candles, which were everywhere. But these candles were the battery-operated kind, the ones on timers. This way, there was always some sort of light in the house when I got home, and it made me feel like someone was there, waiting to welcome me. I had toyed with the idea of getting a pet for company, maybe a cat, but didn't want a cat to feel lonely while I was at work. I actually hated being alone.

I showered quickly and began getting ready for work. Working was pretty much all I seemed to do these days. I was a solitary person, but truly not by choice. Work was the only place I actually had any type of social life, except for any time I got to spend with my best friend Cheryl, and her wife Gina. Cheryl and I worked together, as it were, anyway.

I knew I didn't have any appointments today, so I considered dressing casually. I'm not sure why I even bothered because I struggled with this decision every morning, but could never bring myself to do it. My mother's words would ring in my head, as she always told me how I would be respected more at work if I dressed the part of a professional. I'd always given in. I opted for a black blouse and an ecru skirt with matching pumps. The golden highlights in my dark brown hair seemed to sparkle in the sunlight that was streaming through my bedroom window. It hung in natural loose waves over my shoulders. I applied light make-up, as was my usual routine. My eyes were a very light hue of greenish-blue, so if I globbed on makeup, it looked as though I was heading out for a photo shoot at some swanky magazine. I was more the surfer-girl-next-door-type. I was pretty down-to-earth, yet classy, which was a statement unto itself.

I grabbed a travel mug of coffee, light and sweet, and headed out the door for my semi-short commute. I emerged from my house and the sunlight blinded me. I wasn't sure why. This time of year, the leaves usually blocked the direct sun in the front of my house. It was a pure bright white light and everything erased from my vision for a short time. I quickly covered my eyes, which then caused complete darkness. I wondered if I was having a stroke, because the extremes were so blatant. I tried my best to shake it off. The one thing I always seemed to be able to do was "shake it off." It was an expression my father always used with me when I was young and not feeling well. My dad had been such a huge influence in my life. I missed him terribly. I wished he was still around to continue giving me his words of wisdom and needed advice. He just had a way of making everything seem easy to handle.

When my eyes had completely recovered, I headed for my car. I drove one of those cute mini-coupes and absolutely loved my little black car. It was probably not the safest car due to its size; it sure didn't feel safe when a tractor-trailer was driving next to me on the highway, but I loved it just the same. It was zippy. I parked in my usual spot, and headed into the building while fumbling to get my ID clipped onto the waist of my skirt.

"Good morning, Ms. Porter," the guard said, tipping his hat to me, as I walked through the metal detector.

"Harry, haven't I told you a hundred times *at least*, to call me Sydney?" I kidded with him.

"Yes, Ma'am, but you won't stop and talk to me if I do that." He smiled, and handed back my purse from the x-ray belt.

"I'd talk to you anyway. You're my morning sunshine and one of the only people I know who smiles around here."

"Well, seeing your beautiful face every morning, how could I not smile?" Harry was old enough to be my grandfather, but he was still a huge flirt. He was probably in his mid-seventies. He had gray-peppered hair, and his uniform was always perfectly pressed. His wife must iron it every night. I smiled and shook my head as I aimed toward the elevator.

When I arrived at my office, there was a case file already sitting on my desk waiting for me. *Interesting.* They normally came through via an email alert first. I picked up the file to peruse it while I sipped on my coffee.

Attn: Sydney Porter
New Case Management File
Security Clearance: Highly Classified
Highly Decorated Officer

Included was a hand scribbled note:

This case is to take highest priority.
All of your other cases have been moved to other case managers.
No additional cases will be sent to you.
Appointment scheduled for 10:30 am today. Incoming.

I began to read up on my new *one and only* case. This guy must be someone special, or more likely, be related to someone in the high ranks. Sergeant First Class Aiden Thane. He was seriously decorated, too. He had the Purple Heart, the Army Commendation Medal, the Army Achievement Medal and the Army Distinguished Service Cross. I hadn't met a soldier decorated with all of those medals before. He had no family listed, and no formal education after high school. He seemed to have joined the military right after graduation. In fact, there was really no more information listed, other than his army career. He was being granted an honorable discharge. I'd get the whole story in person from him, I was sure.

With no other work to do until half past ten, I grabbed my coffee, and set off to visit Cheryl, who worked Triple-D (Death Detail Duty) as we called it. It was her task to deal with the dead, those poor souls who never returned from war. She was given lists of all the deceased, waited for their bodies to be delivered home, and then made sure they arrived safely to wherever they needed to go. I was so much happier working with the living. She seemed to prefer working with the deceased, because she didn't have to worry about every soldier hitting on her. Her wife Gina greatly appreciated her work ethic. Cheryl was downright gorgeous. She had shoulder-length, bleached blonde hair and a face that could have any man crouching at her feet. And the gorgeous didn't stop there. It went from the top of her head to the tip of her toes. She was just stunning. Gina was quite the looker, too. She was the tiniest thing, and every movement she made was a bounce full of energy and grace. Her reddish-brown hair was cut into a cute bob, which hugged her petite facial features. She was a dance teacher, which probably explained the bouncy, graceful part. She was a delight in every way; always happy and never a bad word escaped her lips. The only way to describe her would be as angel embodied in human form. You just couldn't help but to be drawn in by her enthusiasm for life.

"Hey, babe, what's happening?" I smiled and said, as I graced the edge of her desk with my backside.

"Oh, I'm doing just great; ten more incoming this morning alone. It's such a shame. All babies, too. Good morning back, by the way. How about you?" She sat back in her chair and put her feet up on her desk, and smiled.

"Well, looks like I've been given a *special assignment*," I said, making quote marks in the air above me. "They pulled all my other cases for this one guy."

"Seriously? What's so special about this one?" Cheryl was the best sounding board for pretty much everything. Since I no longer had my dad, she was my go-to-girl.

"Highly-decorated. You should see the list of medals he has. Other than that, I'm clueless. Guess I'll find out at 10:30; we have a scheduled appointment already." I gave her the double-eyebrow salute. I usually scheduled my own appointments, but this one really was making its own path.

"Well, this should be interesting. I love hearing about all your guys," she teased. She was always pushing me to date, and often with soldiers I worked with.

"Okay, I'll stop back after I meet with him. Are you and Gina still coming for pizza and a horror flick this Friday night?"

"Wouldn't miss it for the world!" she said as she spun her chair around to face her computer. She lazily waved goodbye to me over her shoulder.

"Right. See ya later, babe." I turned and headed back to my office to get all my paperwork in order for my meeting.

Since Cheryl and Gina were my only social life, we had designated every Friday night as pizza and horror flicks at my house. This was not to be confused with Chick-Flick-Sunday, the second Sunday of every month, which was always held at their apartment. We ordered Chinese or Thai food, and made sure we each had our own individual box of tissues. I knew the girls wanted to start a family soon, and were in the process of looking for a house and a good sperm donor, so my time with them as my entertainment was limited. I had to enjoy every little bit. Soon they'd be leaving their little one with Auntie Nini (they had already informed me of my name and future babysitting job). It was fine with me. I loved kids and couldn't wait. It seemed the chances of ever having my own were pretty slim at this point in time.

I often wondered if I would ever find the kind of love they had.

What they possessed was not your *traditional* marriage, but their love was constant, unconditional, and unbreakable. I was sure many people would die for a relationship like they had together. I knew I would, and wanted to find someone but just didn't click with most of the men I met. With me, the connection had to be there from the start. Maybe I was just being too picky. I never threw caution to the wind. In the end, it would probably be my downfall, and I would end up *old spinster Aunt Nini*.

I got back to my office and started to ready forms by filling out what I could. I looked up at the clock and realized I only had a short time before my meeting. I grabbed the paperwork and headed for the elevators.

I hit the button and waited for my ride to the third floor. The door opened and I noticed no one else would be sharing it with me. It was unusual for this time of day, so I leaned back against the wall to relax, watching the doors slide close. The elevator started its ascent and then I felt it bump, heard the motor stop and the lights went out. It was pitch black; not even an emergency light was on. My heart started to race as I felt my way over to the buttons to hit the alarm. Right when I reached them, the elevator jarred back to life. I felt a bit shaken. Getting stuck in an elevator was really not my cup of tea. I giggled with relief when I reached my destination, and the doors opened. I literally leapt out before they had a chance to close, trap me inside and cause my early demise by some freak accident.

I headed over to Incoming to meet my *important soldier*. The third floor was entirely empty. No one was bustling around as usual. *Strange.* This entire day was just not sitting well with me. The place was freezing, too. I was really wishing I hadn't worn my short skirt to work today. I could feel the goose bumps starting to rise on my arms. I peeked down the long empty hallway, and saw one lone man sitting on the benches. He looked like a ghost in a deserted town.

2

AIDEN

"Excuse me, Sergeant Thane?"

The soldier stood up, perfectly at attention, and addressed me with a serious, military tone and utter respect.

"Yes, Ma'am." He offered his hand to shake mine.

My breath hitched in my throat immediately. Any man in uniform was to die for, but he was just drop-dead gorgeous. His dark, messy hair was longer than it should be for someone returning from a tour, and appeared as though he had just rolled out of bed. Sex hair is what I would call it, although others might refer to it as bed head. He must have been at the infirmary for some time. His face was squared and chiseled, and accentuated by a shadow of scruff. His eyes seemed to be piercing right through me. They were a deep shade of blue, but somehow had the appearance they were glowing. I bet now that he was home, all the girls would be knocking down his door, if he didn't have someone already waiting for him. I couldn't imagine he wasn't already spoken for, unless he was a player.

I reached out to shake his hand, and when we touched, I could feel this humming vibration thing happening, from his skin directly to mine. It was reminiscent of something, but I couldn't quite place it. I found myself holding onto his hand a little longer than was socially acceptable for a first meeting but just didn't want to let go. I managed to stutter out a few words.

"Um, hi. I—I'm Sydney Porter. I'll be handling your case." This reaction was so unlike me. No one ever had this type of effect on me.

"Yes, Ma'am," he said, and he released my hand with a small squeeze.

"Maybe you can just call me Sydney, okay? You're making me feel old by calling me ma'am."

"Yes, Ma'am," he said again, but this time, I noticed a small smirk make an appearance at the corner his lips.

"Okay then, great. Would you like to go to one of the meeting rooms to talk for a bit?"

"Ma'am." He nodded his head.

I walked over to the nearest open office, and he followed quietly behind me. He was so silent I couldn't even hear his footsteps. I wondered if he had been trained for covert military missions or was special ops. I showed him to a seat, which he stood behind until I took mine. One thing about soldiers, they were extremely respectful. I loved that.

"So, I see you're being given an honorable discharge. Were you wounded?" I moved my eyes from the file back to his. I found myself looking into them quite often, as I liked the eye contact with him.

"Yes, Ma'am. I was wounded in the line of duty. Shot several times in the chest, four times, to be exact," he said as he continued to stare directly back into my eyes. I wasn't uncomfortable with this at all and I found his presence to be comforting in a strange way. I actually felt a good connection between us already, and we had barely even spoken yet. It made my job much easier when that connection was there. It allowed the soldiers to trust me, more like a friend than a case manager. Somehow this was stronger than I had experience with others.

"I see. That's just terrible. You're very lucky you survived." I averted my eye contact and returned them to my file folder.

"A miracle, I guess," he softly whispered.

"Can I assume the Purple Heart you received is for this injury?"

"Yes, Ma'am."

"And the Distinguished Silver Cross?"

"Yes, Ma'am. I saved my platoon by running cover so they could get to safety." His words seemed uncomfortable for him to say.

"That's very admirable."

He looked down, shying away from my compliment; nodded but said nothing.

"I'm here to help you. I'm going to get you back into the real world, okay? Are there any family members I can contact for you?"

"No, Ma'am."

"No family? How about friends? Anyone at all I can call that you can stay with for a while before we find you a place of your own?"

"No, Ma'am," he said, as he looked down yet again.

"It's fine. I can find you a nice place to stay." I reached out to touch him, but pulled my hand back. The draw I had to him was becoming more intense as the seconds passed by.

He smiled. A man of few words, but I swear I could tell what he was thinking with every movement, smile, or glance we shared.

I started to flip through more of his paperwork, and he began to fidget in his seat. His leg began to twitch up and down, and I could see some slight signs of PTSD emerging.

"Would you like to go get a cup of coffee somewhere? This place is pretty... sterile. There's a great little coffee house right down the street. We can walk there." Sometimes being in the environment wasn't conducive to having them open up to me. They often felt like they were being interrogated. I wanted him to feel more comfortable so he would speak openly.

He looked up and smiled at me. His face was so warm and inviting that I found myself completely taken aback by him. *Damn. All he had to do was smile.* I couldn't help but return the gesture as I stood. He also stood. I was starting to feel as though I was blushing, as I could feel the heat flush my cheeks. This was ridiculous. I had just met this man.

"If you don't mind, I hate carrying my cell phone, and I never hear it ring, so I have this wireless earpiece I use. I just want work to be able to contact me. It's not normal procedure to leave the building." I adjusted the piece into my ear. I hated cell phones becoming fashion accessories. I liked it better when technology didn't follow you everywhere you went. Simpler times.

We walked to the coffee shop and idly chatted about the weather. I talked about how cold it was getting, and he told me how hot it had been where he'd come from. Already the conversation was flowing more easily, and I felt like I had known him for longer than a mere twenty minutes.

The coffee shop was one of my favorite haunts. I frequented it a lot during lunch. It was a comfortable place with large, cushioned chairs instead of the regular shop decor, and there was one of those cool mid-room fireplaces. Sometimes I went there after work, just so I didn't have to return home to an empty house.

We chose a table in the corner, away from everyone else for privacy. I purchased two cups of coffee, and steered myself over to the table to join him. I was actually anxious to get back to him. As I handed him his cup, he gave me that warm smile, and I melted a bit.

"So, we have to find you a place to stay for about a week. There are lots of hotels in the area, the barracks, and a few bed and breakfast places that help us out by taking in soldiers who've just arrived home. Where do you think you'd feel most comfortable?"

"I'm not sure. I've spent a lot of time living the military life.

Honestly I could use a bit of quiet and a break from it, so maybe not the hotel or barracks. I'd love to stay at one of the B&Bs but I'm ..." and then he went silent. I could see he was starting to fidget again; his leg began a reminiscent twitch while he wrung his hands together.

Suddenly, out of nowhere, I just blurted out the words and even shocked myself.

"Would you like to come stay at my place? It's pretty big, and sometimes I feel like I'm just haunting it there all by myself."

He smirked, and cocked an eyebrow at me. He honestly seemed to come alive.

"Are you sure it won't put you out or get you in any type of trouble with work? I don't want you to feel like you have to do this."

"No, no, I want to. I've got a spare room, and it'd be nice to have some company." I couldn't believe I was saying the things that were coming out of my mouth. *Word vomit. What was I doing?* He was a complete stranger. *A highly-decorated soldier stranger. A hot, highly-decorated soldier stranger ... in uniform.* He was becoming seemingly irresistible to me.

"Yes, Ma'am. I'd like to take you up on that offer." His eyes began to burn right into mine. I was now unable to avert my gaze from his.

"Okay. Why don't we go get your belongings?" Now I was taking him to get his things to basically move in with me. *Was I going insane?* I just couldn't resist him. Something about this man pulled me in. It was as though I had known him forever, or maybe we had met before? I had no idea. All I knew was that I just invited this Purple-Heart-toting stranger to stay in the room right down the hall from me. *Oh lord.*

I just smiled at him like a complete idiot.

"I have everything with me." He picked up his duffel bag and pointed at it to show me.

"Maybe we can stop off and pick you up a few things you might need," I offered.

He stared at me. I couldn't take my eyes away from his again. I wondered if my eyelashes were batting.

"I need to get something for dinner, too." This was a true statement. I needed to get supplies for two. My house was honestly set up for only one soul.

"Wait. Let me get this straight. Not only are you offering me a place to stay, taking me to get necessities, but you're also going to cook dinner for me? And I just met you? You're a woman after my own heart," he said smoothly. I had to check the floor for puddles because I melted some more.

I smiled, and a little sigh escaped my mouth as I turned to walk down to the local store with him for some supplies. I was suddenly very aware of every movement I made.

We shopped together like we were an old married couple. We picked out the same colors and similar things. We laughed a lot, and I could only think we had some sort of kismet. I'd heard it said before, that once in a lifetime you met someone who you just completely connected with. Aiden and I were definitely connecting. Could I have just met a man I actually clicked with? I wondered if he was feeling anything close to what I was. The conversation even continued to flow effortlessly on the car ride home. I pointed to various places I thought he might be interested in. *Like I had any idea what interested him. I hope I did.*

When we finally reached my house, I unlocked the door, and offered him entrance. He instead graciously held the door for me. *Soldiers. Gotta love them.* I fumbled with the bags, and he sweetly came to my rescue, dropping his duffel bag at the door, scooping the shopping bags from my arms, and delivering them to my kitchen. We spent some time emptying them together, while I showed him where to locate things at the same time. Soon, everything was done, and I turned to look at my new roommate. It felt right.

"Okay, well, let me show you to ... um, your room. You can get settled in while I start dinner."

"That would be great. Thank you, Sydney." It was the first time he had used my name. It was fine either way, because I would be happy to be 'ma'am' if it was coming from his lips. I blushed a little and turned to head up the stairs. We stopped at the first doorway.

"This is my room. You know, if you want me during the night. *Need. Need me* during the night. Anything you might want. I mean *need*. That ... that I ..." *What was wrong with me?* It was like there was someone possessing me.

"Thanks. Good to know." He smiled as he rescued me from my own inability to spit out my words gracefully. At this point I think he blushed a bit, too. It seemed the attraction *was* mutual, or possibly he thought I was a bumbling idiot. I felt like the latter.

I walked quickly down the hall to the next bedroom.

"This will be your room. The only thing is, we share an adjoining bathroom." I shrugged my shoulders nervously.

"I'll make sure to always knock first before entering." This made me smile, but maybe it was more the thought of him walking in on me during a shower. *Great.* Now I was thinking dirty thoughts about him. I shook my head.

"Me too. Okay, well, I'm going to head back downstairs, down the stairs. I just said that. Okay, well, I'm going now." I walked away slowly, rolling my eyes, and cursing myself for rambling. *If I couldn't even have a small conversation with this man regarding bedrooms and bathrooms, what was I going to be like next?*

I stopped off in my room and changed into comfy clothes. Once I stepped through my front door at the end of the day, I lived in either sweats or skinny jeans; and I preferred to be barefoot. I opted for a cute pair of black boyfriend sweats and a white cami. I refreshed myself with a quick spray of vanilla-scented perfume.

I set off downstairs to quickly set the table, and then was off to the kitchen to begin making dinner.

I started out making the salad, washing the greens and various vegetables. He was suddenly beside me, like he had just materialized there. Startled, I jumped and had to catch my breath. This seemed to make him chuckle.

He was out of his uniform, and dressed comfortably in gray sweatpants and a black t-shirt. He looked amazing even when he was dressed down. I could see his build underneath the thin material of his shirt, and the sweats were hanging just perfectly to make my mind wander.

"I hope I didn't scare you. I'm sure you're not used to someone sneaking up behind you around here. Can I help?"

"No worries. I'm pretty skittish sometimes. And no, you're a guest. I wouldn't ask you to help. Just sit back and relax. I've got it under control." I continued with my dinner prepping. He reached out and put his hand on my forearm.

"Please, let me help you. You're letting me stay with you, so the least I can do is pitch in. I can wield a mean broom," he offered. His voice was so calm and relaxing. It was like listening to an angel.

"How are you with knives?" I asked, hoping for him to take over the task of salad duty, so I could start preparing sauce for the spaghetti. I hated chopping vegetables.

"I'm an expert, Ma'am. Trained in all forms of weaponry."

"I'm not sure if that makes me feel scared or safe." I giggled.

He smiled and reached for my knife. His hand brushed mine, and I felt a quick flutter in my stomach. I looked up at him from under my eyelashes. *Now I was flirting*. I took a step back from him so he didn't think I was some kind of freak, inviting soldiers to stay with me so I could flirt and then have my way with them. In this instance, I wouldn't have minded, though.

He smirked, began chopping carrots and slicing the tomatoes. We cooked the entire meal together. He seemed to be at home in the kitchen, like I was. I loved to cook, and was excited to have, not only someone to cook *for*, but someone to cook *with*.

We dined on our homemade Italian meal with glasses of Merlot, and had the most amazing conversation. I told him about my parents and my childhood. He never mentioned his family so I didn't press him. We talked about the war a lot. We had both experienced it, and it brought us even closer together. We shared something that he couldn't with most other people. It was one of the reasons why I was so good at my job.

When dinner was finished, he thanked me for a home-cooked meal, offering me a bit too much praise, which made me blush again, and then we proceeded to clear the table together.

I grabbed our glasses and an unopened bottle of wine, and we moved over to the couch in my family room. I was really enjoying having company. This might actually turn out to be beneficial for both of us.

I thought it might be a good time to work with him, now that he seemed to be much more at ease. He was still work, no matter how much I was enjoying spending time with him.

"So, can you tell me more about what happened?"

"You mean, why I'm not still over there?"

I nodded. He immediately tensed up and sat straight back against the couch. He looked like a mannequin.

"Not yet. I'm not ready to talk to you about that. Is that okay?"

"It most certainly is. This is on your timeframe. So when you feel more comfortable." I smiled and placed my hand on his to let him know I meant it. We had plenty of time to talk, so I certainly didn't need to rush him. I didn't want to. I needed to take things slowly with him. I wanted him to trust me.

Before I even realized it was happening, we had begun gravitating toward each other on the couch. I'm not sure if it was the wine or the company. It was probably a little bit of both.

He became quiet, and just looked into my eyes. I just couldn't look away. I was lost there. The pull towards him was unstoppable and I felt myself start to lean in his direction. He gravitated back. My breathing became shallow as we inched closer and closer. Soon, we were so close that I could feel his breath on me, and smell the sweet scent of him. I took in a deep breath with the hopes of being able to taste him. He reached up and cupped my cheek.

"You're quite beautiful, you know." I had no words; I couldn't speak and just waited, hoping he would lean in and kiss me first;

and he did. His soft lips pressed against mine, and I felt the familiar humming that happened every time we touched, along with the now fluttering stomach I had recently acquired. I stayed perfectly still; afraid to let myself go. He pulled back and looked at me.

"I'm not going to break, you know. You can kiss me back, if you want to, of course. I can't remember the last time I actually kissed someone. I'm sorry. I don't mean to be so forward and don't even know if you're already spoken for. Hope I'm not overstepping any boundaries."

That was all I needed to hear. I reached up, twisted my fingers into his hair, and pulled his face slowly back to mine without ever breaking eye contact. I kissed him deeply, darting my tongue between his lips. He responded in kind and our tongues began to swirl together. I felt light-headed, but at the same time, I felt completely comfortable. I loved when a man kissed the same way I did. We were completely in sync.

We became lost in our kiss, his hands encircling the back of my neck, holding my face to his; holding us in our kiss. I was in heaven. I moved closer to him so our bodies were touching more. It felt like we had been together for years instead of just having met. We spent some time locked in this embrace, the rest of the world forgotten.

I couldn't believe I was letting this happen, but I had no strength to do anything about it. I wanted it. I wanted him, all of him. I hoped I could find the restraint to stop, since there was just something about this man that made all my defenses and common sense dissolve. Was there truly such a thing as love at first sight? I was teetering on the edge of falling.

Our kisses became deeper, more passionate, and I felt him start to lean me to a more horizontal position. I didn't resist and allowed him to shift me so I was flat on my back. He crawled on top of me and we started to become more aggressive. He began to grind his hips into mine, so my hips responded in kind. I wanted to rip his clothing off, and let him take me, but instead I stopped him. I couldn't believe I did, because I honestly did *not* want to. This entire scenario was so unlike me. I wasn't really a one-night-stand kind of girl.

"Hey, can we just slow down a bit? I'm going to get carried away here, and I don't want you to get the wrong idea. I certainly didn't invite you to stay with me here just for this." I motioned the space between us.

"Sydney, there's no way I could think badly about you. I just know I feel something, and it's a *very strong* feeling. I've never felt anything like this before. Never, not with anyone. I'll do whatever you want me to; I completely understand. But from the moment you walked down that hallway, I just knew this was different; that you were different. I just felt immediately connected to you, like meeting up with an old friend. Does that even make any sense? I don't really want to stop what's happening between us. But we can stop this wonderful foreplay, or maybe just slow down a bit for now," he said openly yet softly into my ear, followed by a sweet kiss on my cheek.

I kissed him while pushing him back slightly, my lips still attached to his. All I was doing now was changing our position back to an upright one. He moved with me, letting me control the situation. He was being a gentleman, even though I was not quite being a lady.

"Would you like to maybe watch TV for while or something? Cards?"

He laughed quietly, and then said, "I was actually really enjoying our most recent activity. Look, I've had a really long day, maybe it would be best if I went up to get some rest."

"Oh my God, of course. Damn it. I'm being so rude. I didn't even think about the fact that you just flew in today. You must be absolutely exhausted. I am so sorry."

"You have nothing to be sorry about. You've been more than wonderful and accommodating to me. This is the most comfortable I've felt anywhere in a long time. Really. Thank you for that."

"Well, I guess we should head up to bed then. I mean, to get some sleep ... in separate rooms," I smiled sheepishly at him. He laughed, ran his hand through his messy hair and then down over his face. He was obviously as worked up as I was, and doing his best to squelch any desire or further action.

"Well, all those things sound great to me." He stood up and offered his hand to help me up from the couch. *Chivalry. Love it.*

We moved up the stairs, and he stopped in front of my door to *drop me off.*

"So, this is a strange place for a good night kiss, especially since we just met today, along with the make-out session downstairs, but here goes." He leaned in and kissed me deeply. I melted into my door, which of course was not shut all the way, and I tumbled backward into my room and away from his lips. He looked a bit shocked, and just stood there like someone had just erased me out of his arms.

"Apparently, fate has a different ending for tonight in mind, so I'll just take that as my cue, and wave from here before I hurt myself." I giggled. I wasn't embarrassed at all; everything felt so natural with him. Normally I would have been mortified to fall into a room during a kiss with someone I just met. Except I never kissed men I had just met ... until Aiden. The whole day had just been so *surreal.*

I lay in bed, thinking about him lying in bed, only a room and a half away from mine. I wondered what he was wearing to sleep. In my mind, he was naked, with just the sheet covering him to his waist. I wondered if he was thinking about me. I couldn't wait to tell Cheryl all about him in the morning. Wait, I didn't have to go to work, as I had no other active cases right now. I'd call Cheryl to meet me for lunch.

When morning came, I was woken by a soft tapping on a door. Aiden must have been checking to see if I was in the bathroom. I looked at the clock. It was only six o'clock. I rolled over to catch a few more minutes of sleep, but found I had butterflies in my stomach at the thought of seeing him.

I literally jumped out of bed to get ready. I didn't hear anything in the bathroom, but I gave it a few soft raps to be sure he wasn't still using it. After no reply, I opened the door so I could take a quick shower and get myself in a more presentable form.

I headed downstairs and could already smell coffee brewing. It smelled heavenly, and I found it completely comforting, because I knew I would have company this morning. I couldn't remember the last time I had eaten breakfast with someone. I found Aiden in the kitchen, reading the morning paper, which he had retrieved from the front porch.

"Good morning. You're still on military time I see." I smiled, and grabbed two mugs from the cabinet.

"Good morning back. I hope you don't mind. I thought you might like coffee. Did I wake you?"

"It's fine, really, I'm not a late sleeper, so no worries," I said, as I casually reached into the fridge for cream, and bread and butter to make toast.

"So I guess you'll need to go to work today?" He sounded a bit disheartened as he said it.

"Actually, no. You're my only case right now. I'm all yours ... for the day," I cleared my throat to cover up my faux pas. "Except maybe for a quick lunch with friends. Do you think you can keep yourself busy while I'm gone?"

"I'm sure I can keep myself amused. I would love to catch up on some TV. I saw you have a pretty extensive library, maybe I'll thumb through one of your books."

I reached into my junk drawer and pulled out my spare key. Again, it should seem strange for me to leave a stranger alone in my house and provide him with the key, but I didn't feel worried.

"You'll be needing this then, in case you go out for a walk or something. Just remember if I come home, and everything is missing, I'll know who it was," I teased.

"Yes, Ma'am, no worries there." He reached out, swiped the key from my hand, and placed it in his pants pocket.

I poured us both coffee and sat down with him at the table. He handed me a section of the paper. I smiled, and took it. We sat in silence, reading the paper, and sipping our coffee like it was old routine with one another. Every once in awhile, one of us would peek over the paper and look at the other, but we always seemed to do it at the same exact time. I found that we both lingered in our stares.

"So, we need to take care of some things for your case. I thought maybe we could sit out back, and just fill out some of the paperwork."

"Yes, Ma'am. Is it okay if I rake your backyard while we do it? Your yard could use it, plus I could use the exercise. I'm feeling a little stiff." A smile spread across both our faces, obviously our minds in sync with the same dirty thought.

I just couldn't believe this. This drop dead gorgeous guy comes into my life, we have instant chemistry, *and* he likes to do housework. Things couldn't get any better. *Could they?*

We headed out to the garage, I handed him the rake, and sent him on his way to get started. I grabbed my cell to call Cheryl to make plans for lunch with her and Gina. When my lunch plans were firmly in place with promises of exciting news to tell them, I headed to my backyard to join Aiden.

I had an expansive piece of property, but part of it was gated from the woods that stretched out behind it, forming a quaint courtyard. There was a creek back there, and often the neighborhood kids could be found playing along the banks. I didn't want them to feel like they were trespassing, so I put the fence up to let them know where their freedom ended on my property. My terrace was constructed in cobblestone, and was adorned with an outdoor sofa, chiminea, and my favorite chair to sit and read in, a large papasan. I settled myself into this chair to watch him work.

He was so muscular, and I was enjoying my view immensely. He raked. I asked questions. He answered. I flirted. He flirted back. We both laughed. He raked some more. Before I knew it, it was time to leave for lunch. Time just didn't exist when I was with him.

"I have to go now. Will you be all right here? Do you want to come with me? I can drop you off at the base so you can take care of anything you might need to there. Or if you'd like, you can join us for lunch."

"No, thank you. I'll be just fine here. I'd like to finish up the yard. Do you mind if I do some other things around here? I noticed they could use a man's touch."

"Be my guest. I *love* you." Immediately, I realized that my innocent comment might sound totally out of line. My eyes got wide, I felt the blood drain from my face, and my mouth dropped open but nothing came out.

"Good to hear." He gave me that amazing smile, and any strangeness was suddenly at a zero level. He leaned in to kiss me gently. *Hum and tingle.*

Aiden walked me to my car, and watched as I pulled down the drive. He looked lost when he waved goodbye to me. He was out of sight in a moment, and I strangely found myself missing him already. I definitely thought about him the entire drive to lunch, feeling like I was in high school with a crush on a cute boy.

3

CHERYL

I was driving to a local diner, which I frequented with my girls at least once a week. It was close to Gina's ballet studio, so Cheryl and I join her there often for lunch or dinner.

When I arrived I searched for them. They were sitting in the back in the greenhouse room, so it took me a few minutes to locate them. Gina liked to sit where it was sunny; she didn't like to feel closed in.

She was sitting very close to Cheryl. It was so obvious they were a couple. I'm sure there were people at the diner, and other places, who had issues with their relationship. That always infuriated me. They were one of the sweetest, most down-to-earth couples I knew. Their relationship had outlasted many of the heterosexual ones I knew. Their marriage was forever, whatever *that* meant. I was positive if there were an afterlife, you'd find them together even then. I sometimes wished everyone would just stop all the prejudice. It seemed to me that everyone should be past it by now.

"Hello, ladies. Am I late?"

"Hi, Sydney!" Gina pulled me into a hug and planted a kiss on my cheek.

"No, you're right on time. I ordered you a diet with a twist of lime, just like you always order." Cheryl knew what women wanted. That's exactly how she swept Gina right off her feet. The second they met it was true love-at-first-sight. Their chemistry oozed out of them, and there was no way anyone could overlook it. They had been with each other for many years now, yet the bond was still as strong as ever. I wondered if what I felt for Aiden was even remotely close to what they had experienced when they had first met.

"So no office time for you anymore?" Cheryl questioned me like she was my mother.

"I only have *one case*. Why go into the office?" I sounded just like her snarky teenager in my reply.

"So, who is this guy, a general's son?" I could see Cheryl was going to grill me on everything today.

"No, nothing like that. He's this very handsome decorated soldier."

"Handsome. Hmm." Gina's eyes gleamed when she said it, and she shot Cheryl a cute look.

"I didn't say handsome. I said *highly*. *Highly* decorated soldier."

"No, you didn't, you said handsome. I heard you." Gina voice was sing-songy, like a young child ready to start singing the *kissing in a tree* song.

"Cheryl, please tell her I said highly. Please make her stop."

"Sorry, I can't do that. You said handsome." Cheryl had an evil grin on her face. It was Gina and Cheryl's favorite game. They had a blast messing with me. I didn't mind one bit because I laughed a lot when I was with them. They were the closest thing to family I had these days.

"Okay, he *is* handsome."

"How handsome?"

"He's gorgeous!" I proceeded to tell them all about his body, face, hair, everything I could possibly think of. I wanted to let Cheryl hear how easily we got along, because I knew she was going to be concerned. Although she often suggested dating soldiers, she was still very protective of me. She really was like a stand-in mother at times, or more so like an older sister. She needed to hear how we clicked instantly. I rambled excitedly for quite some time.

"So where's he staying? Somewhere close by?" Cheryl questioned.

"Yeah, about that." This little tidbit of information was something I knew would freak her out.

"Is there an issue with where he's staying? I bet if I spoke to our landlord he'd be happy to put him up in one of our units. Joe's a veteran; he'd be more than happy to help out another vet. I know there are a couple of the smaller units available and I can call him right now if you want."

"No, it won't be necessary. He's staying with me." I looked down so I couldn't see Cheryl's eyes burning into me, along with flames shooting out her nostrils. This was *not* going to go over well.

"Are you fucking kidding me? You don't know anything about this guy!"

"I know, Cheryl, but please understand, there's something about him. It's just there, between us. It's a really strong connection. I felt it the second we met."

"Wow, Sydney, are you out of your mind? You have no idea what he's like. He could be all messed up in the head from the war. Please let me call Joe and we can get this guy out of your place today."

"Cheryl, correct me if I'm wrong, but didn't you take Gina home with you the first night you met? She stayed the whole damn weekend. A month later you were living together."

"That's different. Look at her."

"You haven't seen him yet. It's *not* different."

"I think it's sweet. Lighten up, Cher. This guy could be her *me*," Gina chirped.

"Aiden is amazing. I actually can't wait to get back to see him. It's insane." I addressed only Gina.

"It's insane, all right. This guy could be a predator. You left him alone at your house? What if he steals everything or goes through your things?" Cheryl was pissed.

"He's a war hero. He wouldn't do that!"

"Because you know him so well? Remember that story from a few years ago? The one about that soldier who also happened to have a Purple Heart? The whole town celebrated him as a hero, with a parade and everything. A week later, he had committed suicide. No one had any idea he wasn't the person he used to be or that he was suffering silently. Even his family had no idea he was hurting so badly. Post Traumatic Stress Disorder does things to people. No one is helping the soldiers deal with it. There should be screening or groups to help them open up about it. It's not even like you knew Aiden well before he left for the war so you could notice a change. You just met him yesterday. How can you confidently say he wouldn't do something?"

"I ... I can't. Remember, Cher, I *am* a psychologist. I'm sure I would recognize all the signs."

"So you saw no signs of any PTSD?"

"No." That was an outright lie. Every soldier had some form of it. I had seen a few moments yesterday. Aiden seemed to withdraw inside himself each time I noticed, though, and he didn't come across to me as a threat.

Gina began to jokingly lay into Cheryl about backing off, and letting me finally enjoy being with someone. I half listened as she basically called me her *potentially lost cause*, who might have a shot at some kind of relationship, no matter how long it lasted. I should have been insulted. Why did she think I would never find anyone? Maybe I wasn't the only one who really thought I'd end up a spinster. I felt like their child, sitting at the table while they talked about me like I wasn't even there.

The other half, the one not listening, began to have an anxiety attack. Cheryl was right. I didn't know this man at all. I invited a complete stranger, who even the United States government had little or no known background on, to live at my home. What if he wasn't who I perceived him to be? Did I actually make him out to be someone I wanted, just because I was looking for it? He could be a cold-blooded killer or a crazed maniac, and he was at my house alone with all my things. At this point in time, he could be looking through my computer for all my personal information or stealing all my jewelry. I felt a cold sweat break out on my forehead.

"Hun, are you okay? You're not looking so good right now." Gina reached up as she said it and felt my forehead like the great mom she was going to be to her future kids.

"I'm good." The pit in my stomach and the lump in my throat said differently. I wanted to jump in my car to rush home to check on Aiden.

"Syd, did I just ruin everything for you with your new man? I'm sorry. I just worry about you. It's bad enough I worry about you being alone all the time in those woods that surround your house, but now, add a complete stranger that I've never met to the mix. I'm just looking out for you."

"You scared the shit out of her, Cher. Stop it. Let her enjoy falling in love without all the drama. I'm sure everything will be fine. Why don't you tell me more about him, Sydney," Gina requested.

"I don't know if I would go to the extreme of saying I'm falling in love. He's a very sweet man and the potential is there. Heck, right now he's working in my yard."

"A man that does yard work is a plus. Tell me more. It'll make you feel better again," Gina said.

"He cooked dinner with me last night, and we never ran out of things to talk about the entire time. He got up and made me coffee this morning." I sounded like I was trying to convince all three of us that he was a good guy.

"Did he bring it to you in bed?" Cheryl was not going to let this go. Gina shot her a dirty look and I swear I heard her mumble 'no sex for you tonight' under her breath.

"No," I said flatly.

"Well, was there *any* nookie last night?" Cheryl questioned.

I really didn't want to tell her how we made out on the couch. At the same time, I really wanted to get all giddy over it with Gina.

"Does kissing count?"

"Who are you and what did you do with my prudish friend Sydney?" Cheryl said, rolling her eyes.

"Yay! You kissed him. Is he a good at it?" Gina was full of enthusiasm. I wished I had only met with her for lunch.

"I don't want to hear about her kissing him. If it was a hot chick, maybe."

"Shut up, Cheryl. Just ignore her, Sydney. Tell me. I want to hear all about it. Did he give you soft gentle kisses? Was there tongue involved?" Now both Cheryl and I rolled our eyes. It was like I was in the cafeteria in high school.

"Yes, Gina. We French kissed. He touched my boobs, too."

"Over or under the shirt?" Gina liked her details.

"Are you kidding me? We do *not* need to hear about that. That's all, though, right?" Cheryl quizzed.

"I stopped him. I was seriously going to let him do whatever he wanted, but I didn't want him to think I was easy."

"Oh no, nothing easy about a girl who invites you back to her house the first day you've met … to live with her."

"Cheryl, you know I'm not like that."

"I'm not sure what you're like. This whole thing is completely out of character for you. Might I add it's also not ethical? Where is your work professionalism? It anyone finds out, you'll lose your job."

"The only people who know are you two and Aiden. I'm quite confident none of you are going to say anything."

"His name is Aiden? That's such a nice name. That's a Gaelic name and it means little fire."

"Gina, how the hell do you know that?"

"She's been in the baby name books again. It's nonstop lately."

"That's so wonderful. Do we have a plan yet for who the donating father will be?"

"Not yet. We're still looking. It's a really hard decision," Gina replied.

"Please don't get her started."

"It's fine. I won't get all teary anymore. I'm just looking for the right guy. Speaking of which, let's get back to Aiden and kissing."

"He's a great kisser and a complete gentleman. But let's not get Cheryl all fired up again, shall we?" But it wasn't Cheryl I was worried about. All sorts of scenarios were now running through my head about Aiden.

We spent the rest of lunch just plain bullshitting, which was our normal mode of conversation. After we had finished, I gave them both a hug and peck on the cheek, so I could head back home as fast as I could … home to Aiden. The butterflies were already starting. But were they good butterflies or bad ones? I really had no idea anymore. The realization of what I had actually done by inviting him to stay with me was hitting home thanks to Cheryl. I loved her for opening my eyes to everything I would not normally think about. This, however, was something I should have considered carefully first.

I'd have to learn to think before I blurted various things out to him. He had a way of making our conversations just flow so easily.

My drive home was not as pleasant as my drive out. Why did Cheryl always have to be so leery about everyone? Instead of being excited about getting back to Aiden, now I was apprehensive. I was not happy about that feeling at all.

4
AIDEN

When I pulled into the driveway, I was amazed at how much he had gotten done. My yard was raked, my rose bushes trimmed for the winter, and generally, everything was pruned and preened. My garage door was open and I could tell it had been straightened out. Wow, he really did wield a mean broom. The floor was spotless and the shelves completely organized.

All my concerns during the drive home seemed to suddenly disappear. He wasn't *up to no good* while I was gone, he was working his ass off.

I shut the door and headed inside to find him. He was in my kitchen with a handful of dishes, cleaning up from lunch.

"Hey," I sort of purred at him.

"Good afternoon, Sydney. Did you have a nice time?"

"Yes, we always have a very good time when we're together."

I needed to do something to make myself feel better about the conversation I had over lunch. I needed to touch him. So I walked right up to him, grabbed his face and kissed him. He seemed slightly surprised, but didn't pull away.

"All I could think about was getting home to do that. Is that wrong? Am I going insane?" He smiled, reached out to wrap his arms around me, and pulled me into him. He buried his face into my shoulder and hair. The scent of him was intoxicating for someone who had just spent the last few hours probably sweating. He smelled sweet. I felt comfortable in his arms and didn't want to let him go.

"If it's insane, then I'll be in the padded room right next door to yours. I'm relieved to hear you're feeling the same way. I thought I was losing it. I was afraid I might scare you off or intimidate you."

If he only knew it was Cheryl who was scaring me. I almost felt guilty thinking so wrongly about him. How could I do that? I was so easily swayed and felt like I had somehow betrayed him. I put my head down because I couldn't bear to look him in the eyes.

He took a step back from me and caressed my cheek and pulled my face up to meet his gaze.

"Is everything all right?" His blue eyes burned into mine, and I found myself getting lost in them, as usual. It seemed like all that existed was he and I at that moment. I wasn't even aware of the room we were standing in anymore. It was almost like we were in a time warp of some kind or a bubble.

"Everything is just fine. I was thinking about something my friend said."

"Well, you certainly didn't look very happy. Was it bad news?"

"Nothing like that. It's all good. I see you were very busy while I was gone. You did so much," I said, trying to change the subject.

His face lit up as he took my hand and led me out to the backyard to show me his handiwork and all he had accomplished back there as well.

"I tried to make sure to keep your Zen back here, if not increase it. You obviously had some already. I know I like a space to feel warm and inviting no matter where it is. I noticed some old candles, lanterns and wind chimes in the garage, and I thought they'd work back here. I bet you spend a lot of time hanging outside when it's nice. This is how I would want it. I hope I didn't overstep my bounds. I can put it all back the way you had it if I did."

The entire terrace had been rearranged. My papasan chair and its dark blue cushion were now a focal point, instead of being off to the side. He had arranged the furniture around my outdoor fireplace, which I had actually never used, but I could see it was all ready for its first fire. The chiminea was now filled with candles instead. The lanterns and candles resided everywhere. He had even cleaned out the small water feature pond I had, and the small waterfall was working again. Everything was trimmed and tidy. The yard looked amazing. The breeze that was blowing made my wind chimes ring softly. It was all very soothing. It had been my original plan to utilize these things to de-stress before I went to bed at night, but I had never had the time nor energy to do it properly. He had completely achieved what was in my head, which was feng shui.

"I just saw all these things you obviously had plans to do something with, and I felt bad they weren't being used. I wanted you to have everything just right. Did I get it right?"

"Hell yes. It's perfect. I mean it, too. I love it. You really did too much and I can't thank you enough."

"I'm really the grateful one. You're a very sweet person. It wasn't really that big of a deal. The yard was in good shape and it didn't really take me much time at all."

"But you did my garage and out front, too. Really, you did so much. I can't get over it. Do you wield a magic wand, too? You have mad skills at landscaping."

Aiden genuinely smiled. I was glad I made him happy. He had spent the entire afternoon working like a dog on my yard and he didn't have to. I did feel a bit more comfortable knowing he had been busy all day. I almost felt guilty for thinking badly about him for even a second today.

"I felt like I knew what you would like. It was so easy. It just fell together, honestly. I went with my gut feeling. It's weird. I feel like I've known you for longer than a day."

"I know, right? I feel so connected to you. Like we're on the exact same plane."

"Yeah, something like that. Absolutely."

This was all so out of character for me. But maybe this was what falling in love was supposed to be like. I had no idea, as I had never actually fallen for someone like this before. And the best part was that it seemed to be mutual. I suddenly realized I had thought about falling in love with him. Maybe Gina had been right after all.

"Would you like to try it out tonight when the sun goes down? I'd like to make sure I got the lighting perfect. Maybe we could even have a fire in the chiminea."

"I'd love that. I'm out here almost every night during the summer. I love to read back here. It's so peaceful."

"Peaceful. That's a wonderful thing to feel. That's what I was going for. It's a very hard thing to achieve, you know. Especially in the world we live in these days. Everyone is so absorbed in their own little life, they don't see the big picture."

"What do you think the big picture is?"

"I think it's not on this earth. I think whatever exists after this life is what really matters. But maybe that's because of everything I've been through. It all seems so ridiculous to worry about what kind of car you drive or what meeting you have coming up. Inevitably, we all end up in the same place, right? One that's completely different than this life we're living now."

"That's very profound. I guess you might be right. I don't know. Not sure what I believe in these days. I guess it's everything I've experienced.

We continued our conversation, while enjoying my newly spruced up terrace. Time flew by, and before we knew it, we were inside cooking dinner again. Everything was so easy between us. It was all so natural. It was all so strange.

After a nice dinner and a quick cleanup of dishes, we retired to my cushy couches to watch a movie. I thought a war-based movie would be a good one for us to watch together, so we could analyze if it was realistic or not. And it might make him open up to me about what he had gone through during his tour.

We cuddled up close, our glasses of wine in hand, and started to watch. He put his arm around my shoulder and I snuggled into his side. I was safe and comfortable and felt as though we had been with each other for years.

Within the first twenty minutes of the movie, we watched as the first soldier died. Aiden's body immediately began to shudder. He seemed almost like he was in some kind of trance. He went catatonic. *Holy crap, I should've known better than to bring his memories back to war and death.* It was completely out of line for me and I was certainly not thinking like an experienced psychologist.

"Aiden, are you okay? Aiden, can you hear me?" I jumped up, and tried to shake him out of it.

He had no reply. Instead he just stared right past me as though I was not in the room with him. His eyes squinted and then his face took on a look of terror. The corner of his mouth started to twitch. If I didn't know better, I would have thought he was about to have some sort of a seizure. But in a few moments, I realized that he seemed to be reliving the moments when he had been wounded. I saw him mouth the words 'Oh shit, no' and then his body bucked and flailed four times like he was being shot. I watched him in horror.

I started to panic and grabbed his shoulders and tried to steady him. His eyes rolled into the back of his head and he went completely limp. This was bad, very bad. I considered calling for an ambulance, but I was afraid to leave his side. The phone seemed so far away.

"Oh my God, Aiden. Snap out of it. You are okay. Can you hear me? Just open your eyes. I'm right here in front of you. I won't let anything happened to you. You're safe now. You're with me now. I'm right here. Can you feel me? I just need you to try and shake this off."

Cheryl's words echoed in my head. I started to doubt myself, and this whole situation. *What had I gotten myself into? What had I done to him?*

I put my hands on either side of his face. His skin felt cold and clammy. Soon his eyes began to move underneath his lids. He took in a deep gasp of breath like he hadn't been breathing at all for the entire episode. Then he opened his eyes. I felt a wave of relief wash over me.

"Aiden? Please tell me you're okay. Please talk to me. Just say something so I know you're all right."

"Sydney, I'm so sorry. I didn't want you to ever see that." He seemed to have his wits about him now.

"That's happened to you before?"

"I have ... um, nightmares, I guess you could call them. They're very similar to what just happened, except you weren't there when I snapped out of it." He touched my cheek and ran a fingertip down until his hand was over my heart. He left it there, as if he was feeling every single beat. Of course my heart completely complied by beating faster and harder at his touch. My entire body reacted to his touch. It seemed to be reviving him. With each thump of my heart, the color returned to his face.

"Listen, you still look really pale. You're shaking. Do you want a glass of water? Do you want to maybe go lay down?"

"Will you come with me?

I had to stop and think this over carefully. What exactly was he asking of me? I didn't want him to be alone. If that type of event happened again, I wanted to be by his side to make sure he was fine. That was not something I wanted him to ever experience alone again.

Being by his side would also make me not want to leave him for the rest of the night. I had already decided I wasn't going to let anything happen between us this evening. I was putting myself at risk because knew I wouldn't be able to hold back if things progressed sexually between us again. I couldn't even believe I was thinking about him sexually right now. My mind was already made up because I blurted out my answer.

"Of course." *Damn, I was my own worst enemy.* I helped him to his feet and up the stairs. His episode downstairs seemed to have totally drained the life from him. He was weak and still very pallid. I brought him to his room and helped him over to his bed.

"Listen, you overdid it today. First working in the yard all day. And then I was a complete idiot to pick that movie. That's all. I'm going to get you a glass of water and an aspirin, and give you a minute to get changed. Then I want you in that bed, Mister."

My last statement made him smile. That was a very good sign. I left to get his water and an aspirin. When I returned he was sitting up on the bed waiting for me. My mind started wandering because he looked hot as hell in his present location. I tried to avert my eyes so as not to appear to be leering at him, but it was impossible.

"Okay, take this and a sip of water." He held out his hand and I dropped the pill into it.

"Thanks."

"All right. I think you should lie down and take it easy. Do you want something to help you sleep?"

"No, I don't want to take anything that'll knock me out. What if you needed me during the night?"

So this man just had some sort of episode and he was thinking about my wellbeing?

"That's very sweet. Okay. I'm going to head to bed, too. Can I have a rain check for that outside fire?"

"Absolutely." I laid him down and tucked him in. I turned to leave, and he grabbed a hold of my hand.

"Sydney, please stay with me, at least for a little while. Until I fall to sleep. I don't really want to be alone right now. Is that asking too much of you?"

"No, of course not. I'll stay as long as you want me to."

"Would you stay the night?" he said it so quietly, I could barely hear him.

Now normally I would have been nervous, or jumping up and down like an idiot. But right now all I wanted to do was hold him, and comfort him as much as he needed. I slid in beside him with a smile and a little bit of fluttering in my stomach. He lifted up the covers to invite me closer to him. I did so without hesitation and curled up next to him, nuzzling my face into his chest. He wrapped his arms around me.

The feel of his skin against mine was starting to make me want to rub myself all over him. My body definitely had other things in mind than just lying beside him, but I was also just as content to feel his body against mine.

His body was cool, so I snuggled in even closer to keep him warm. Where my body touched his, it hummed and then warmed. I couldn't sleep. I hated sleeping in my clothes and I was fully dressed at the moment. I also wanted to make sure he was going to be all right. Not to mention, of course, being beside him was still making my heart palpitate.

It wasn't long before he was out. He slept like the dead. He didn't move an inch. I'm not sure how long I was awake watching him sleep but eventually I drifted off to dreamland.

It had been at least a few hours into the night when I felt the bed shake me awake. He was probably having a nightmare. I tried to wake him, but he only became silent again at my touch and the sound of my voice when I whispered his name. I thought this would be a good time to put something more comfortable on and hit the bathroom. While I was away, I heard him cry out. I didn't hear him say anything definitive because everything sounded muffled through the door. I hurried back to his side and climbed back into bed with him, and he immediately quieted again. I curled myself around him, and we spent the rest of the night without any further events.

5
CHERYL

I let Aiden sleep in, sneaking out of bed before the sun had risen. I watched him for a moment before I left, and realized how quickly I was becoming attached to him. I needed to talk to Cheryl again and wanted to use her as a sounding board. She'd be painfully blunt, and let me know exactly how to slow things down. I put on coffee, and figured I would wait until it was a reasonable time to call.

I decided to check out my newly renovated Zen in the back yard. The terrace stone was frigid on my bare feet as I stepped outside. The days were getting colder lately. I knew it was only a matter of time before winter would be approaching. I disliked winter greatly and had often entertained the idea of moving somewhere that always hovered around seventy to seventy-five degrees. That was my ideal temperature.

The morning was extremely quiet. Not a single bird made a sound. I could actually hear the creek babbling in the distance, somehow amplified by the stillness of everything else. It was so peaceful. I almost thought about waking Aiden so he could share this time with me, but I knew he needed the rest. So I dismissed the idea.

I decided to grab my coffee and a blanket to spend some time by myself, rummaging through all the various conundrums in my head. I plopped myself into my papasan, swaddled, clinging to my cup of joe for warmth, and watched the sunrise. It had been awhile since I had actually appreciated the beauty of it. *Why hadn't I spend more of my time enjoying the simple pleasures of life?* I was always so preoccupied with work or what bills needed to be paid. It seemed like such a waste of time right now. I should have been taking advantage of all the beauty around me. Aiden was the reason for my change of thought and heart. He made everything seem so much more vivid and real. A simple smile or a gentle touch, things I hadn't been paying attention to recently because they didn't exist and were not the things I had been searching for, were all that I craved. *Why was he suddenly changing my priorities and viewpoints in my life, and in such a short time?*

The sun slowly brought a rosy glow to my Zen, but no warmth came with it. I thought of Aiden, cozy in bed, only seconds away from me, and wondered if heading back to snuggle with him was my best option. *Would he remember his nightmare from the middle of the night? Would things be awkward between us?* Nothing had happened, not that I didn't think about rolling over to start something a few times throughout night. It was too soon.

This was not the relationship I thought I had wanted. I wanted the courting; the emails and texts, getting ready for a date and having him pick me up at the door. This was not a possibility when you were living with someone you wanted to be in the beginning of a relationship with. The start of a relationship was one of the best parts. I loved the first kiss and butterflies in your stomach at seeing that other person. I had the first one with Aiden. The second was not as easy due to our location proximity. I still had fleeting moments of them, though.

Then there was the first intimate encounter, the first time

making love to each other. I wanted that to be because Aiden and I felt deeply for each other, not because we were hanging out on the couch and things progressed too hot and heavy with no one heading home for the night. It was too easy to let that happen between us. I needed to get to know him better and to think rationally about what was happening here. I knew nothing about him. He could be using me. He could actually feel what I was feeling. I wasn't sure, and I hated feeling wishy-washy and unsure. It was so easy to do right now. My head said one thing, my heart another, and my hormones were doing their own thing, too. All three fought with each other.

I needed my sounding board now, no matter how much she was going to rip into me about it. I wanted it and needed a dose of reality to set myself straight. I knew it was still early, but Gina was an early riser, so maybe I might catch them both awake.

I listened to the first two rings, considered hanging up to wait for a more decent hour to call, and then someone answered.

"Hello?" It was Gina, sounding like she had been up for hours already. She was already chipper.

"Hey, Gina. Sorry if I'm calling too early."

"Good morning, Sweetie. Don't worry about it. I've been up for awhile. Cheryl is in the shower right now, so you didn't wake either of us up. How are things going with Sergeant Hot Stuff?"

"Oh, Gina, it's amazing. I mean really, it's been so intense. It's all so confusing. I don't even know if this is real or not."

"Of course it's real. That's what it was like with Cheryl and me. I knew it the minute I saw her that she and I were meant to be forever."

"I feel something like that, too. Did you have any doubts that first weekend you spent with her? Were you scared?"

"I wasn't scared of her, if that's what you mean. Are you afraid of him hurting you?"

"No, nothing like that. It's just I reacted when I met him. I didn't even realize what I had done when I invited him to stay with me. I just blurted it out. I haven't thought any of this through."

"Are you having regrets? It's been what, two days?"

"Yeah, something like that. It's all just blurring together, like he's always been here. It's strange. It's happening way too fast. Maybe."

"*Maybe* he's your soul mate or you knew each other in a past life. You know I believe that we've all met each other in our past lives. It's why you feel familiarity with certain people. They were someone important to your last existence. I'm sure you and I were friends or possibly related in a previous life. It explains déjà vu quite nicely, too."

Gina was a strong believer in reincarnation. We had talked about it a few times during drunken nights, when Cheryl had surpassed her limit of drinks and passed out. Gina was a mystical soul, stating with no reservations and complete confidence, that she and Cheryl had loved each other through *many* previous lives. She equated the ease of their relationship with already knowing who Cheryl was, and just returning to what had already existed, but had been on hold when one lifetime ended until the next had begun. She believed they would find each other no matter what the circumstances, should a new existence begin. She said it was why it didn't matter if they were opposite sexes or the same. *Were Aiden and I past life lovers?* I had dabbled in the thought of reincarnation before, always hoping to find out if there was more to come after this life ended.

"Yes, you were my mother and Cher was my father," I teased.

"Probably. That's why she's so protective of you." Gina had taken my joke quite seriously.

"Thanks for liking my new boyfriend, Mom." I guess in my head, Aiden and I were already in a committed relationship. I sounded pathetic to myself and couldn't believe I was entertaining thoughts us being in a relationship. I had no idea if he felt the same way I was.

"Boyfriend. I'm so happy to hear you say that." I guess Gina had no problem with my defining Aiden's role.

"But, Gina, it's all happening so fast."

"Just sit back, go with the flow and enjoy the ride, Syd. It could end tomorrow, a year from now, or never. So enjoy every little bit of it. No one knows what life has in store for him or her, so why waste it worrying about it instead of living it? Am I right?"

"You're so damned down-to-earth and logical. I need to just let things happen. I over think things all the time. That's my biggest downfall."

"I'm glad to hear you say it out loud. Now I want to see you actually do it. I'm so happy for you. I can't wait to meet him."

"I'm afraid. Not of you, you're a doll. I'm afraid of introducing him to Cheryl. She's already upset about him living with me. She'll scare him away."

"No, she won't. Don't be silly." Gina giggled. "Her bark is worse than her bite. You know that. As soon as she meets him, and sees how happy you are, she'll be on board with this whole thing. Just wait, you'll see."

I heard the phone jumble around, and then it was Cheryl on the other end. Cheryl would put everything into perspective for me. She would give me the pros and cons unbiasedly. I'd have plenty of food-for-thought and I could stop fighting with myself in my head.

"I told you not to encourage her, G. Sydney, are you okay? Is everything all right?"

"Everything is fine. My things are all where I left them, except for some leaves and weeds."

"Okay, good. Well, I'm not on the approval-bandwagon yet. I think you need to slow things way down." There was Cheryl's bluntness coming through. It was only a matter of time before she opened up and *really* let me know how she felt.

"But I'm happy. I mean, this guy, he's different. I just feel so much for him already. It's been such a short time but we're already so connected. It's just happening all on its own." I knew I didn't need to get her approval, but I did want her to accept him.

"It's been two days, Sydney, and not even full days yet. That's insane. What are you going to do when he's done with you?" Cheryl was asserting her big sister or motherly side. It didn't matter; it was all the same to me. I had asked for her opinion by calling, so I needed to be ready to hear what she had to say and accept it or not.

"It's not like that. He feels the same way I do." I pouted.

"And how is that exactly, Sydney?"

"We both feel very strongly for each other."

"And he told you that?"

"Not in so many words."

"So you're assuming he feels the same way? What if this is all one-sided?"

"Don't be silly. He's let me know he's as interested in me, just as much as I am in him," I said convincingly.

"When are you going to realize that it could all just be a novelty, Sydney? If it is, it's going to wear off. You just can bet on it. Wait until he gets settled back into his real life. You might not be needed anymore."

"I don't understand what you're saying. What do you mean a novelty?" I could feel my blood pressure starting to rise.

"You don't *want* to understand, Syd. You're just not thinking over the logistics of this whole thing. He had a life before the military, and it's going to rear its ugly head somewhere down the line and probably when you least expect it. You'll be tossed to the side with nothing but heartache. Do you really think he's going to choose you over the life he had before? Are you prepared for that? The whole idea of what's happening between you, it's like meeting a cute guy on spring break. You have a great time together, you promise to keep in touch, but when you get home it's all forgotten. Be ready in case this isn't going to last."

And that was about all I could take. "You're ... you're wrong!

How do you know that? Maybe I'm the one he's meant to be with. Maybe he'll choose me. I swear to God, you'll see, Cheryl. Can't you just believe in me for once? Why can't I be the girl with the fairytale ending? Is that so hard for you to accept? I have to go," I snapped at her and hung up.

How could she think that? Did she honestly think I was worth so little to someone? It was not only an insult to Aiden's morals, but to my self worth. Right now, all I wanted to do was rush to Aiden's side. Feeling him next to me would make everything better. Her words echoed in my head as I slowly climbed the stairs to get to Aiden.

6

AIDEN

I stood on the other side of his door, debating on whether or not I should enter. A strange thought crossed my mind, that he wasn't going to be there when I opened it. That this had all been some strange dream, and he never really existed. A lump formed in my throat as I finally secured the guts to open the door. He was wrapped in the covers with his back to me. If I snuck in quietly, he probably wouldn't even know I had left.

I tiptoed to *my side* of the bed, smiling to myself that I had referred to it that way in my head.

I eased my body back under the covers, propped my head on my hand and just watched him snooze for a while. He really did sleep like the dead, not even stirring at the motion of my climbing back in bed with him. His eyes moved back and forth under his lids and I was pretty sure he was dreaming. *Was he dreaming about me?* I hoped he was. A sweet smile spread over his face, and I convinced myself he actually was thinking of me. I edged closer to him. I wanted to reach out and touch him, so I did. Leaning over, I gently kissed his lips. His eyes fluttered open in response.

"Good morning," I purred.

"It is now. That's the nicest alarm clock I've ever had."

"I'm sorry I woke you. You were sleeping so peacefully and you obviously needed to catch up."

"Don't apologize. I'd rather be awake and spending time with you. It looks as though you've been up for awhile. I hope I didn't snore or kick you."

"No, don't be silly." He obviously didn't remember his second episode, and I thought it best not to mention it right now. He leaned in so his mouth was right against my ear. Waves of warmth and tingles from him being so close washed over me.

"I'm sorry about last night. It's not how I imagined our first night *sleeping* together would be," Aiden whispered into my ear, his voice sounding slightly embarrassed, yet still in good spirits.

"You've thought about that?" I was shocked. *I thought it was just my little fantasy.* I felt badly he was upset about it. It didn't really bother me at all, and I was happy I hadn't mentioned it to Cheryl.

"I'm sorry. It's wrong of me. We've just met. I'm being way too forward. Forgive me. I don't even know if you're thinking the same way I am."

I was too quick to answer him but I needed him to know. "No, I feel the same way. We keep stumbling across this same thing, this connection we have. I think we're beyond feeling like we're being forward and apologizing for it."

"Agreed." He reached out, grabbed my shoulders and pulled me down to him. We lay face to face with our arms and legs entwined. Everything about the phone call jumped out of my head. All that mattered was right here, right now, with Aiden.

"So, I was thinking. We actually haven't had a proper date. If I'm going to allow things to continue at this pace, I need you to know that I want to give you everything, not just an attraction, and you're letting me stay here with you. Don't get me wrong, this has been wonderful, but I want to show you that you mean more to me. And I want you to enjoy having someone pursue you. You deserve to be treated the proper way. Would you like to go to the park while it's still nice out and maybe have a picnic? The weather reports I watched yesterday said we're in for some bad ice storms later in the week."

It was like he had read my mind. I know I hadn't mentioned those thoughts on the phone with Gina or Cheryl, so he didn't overhear me say anything to them. We were just on the same page. My heart did a little flip in my chest.

"I'd really enjoy that."

"I know you must have other work you need to attend to, so you let me know when a good day is."

"Nope, I told you before, you're it. A day in the park would be working for me. Today would be absolutely perfect." I smiled and placed a soft kiss on his lips.

"I want a job just like yours, so I can kiss you all day long. Think you can help me find one?"

"I'd probably get fired if anyone knew we were kissing, let alone your staying here with me."

"Well, can we just not tell anyone? I don't want you to get fired, but I don't really want to be away from you, either. I feel very *drawn* to you, like I can't be anywhere else but with you. Right here, right now," he confessed to me.

"I really feel the same way. It's crazy, right?"

"It's rather surreal. Things like this only happen in the movies. It's definitely not normal reality. It just doesn't happen on a daily basis, and rarely ever lasts an eternity." He had a serious expression on his face.

"Oh, I ... We don't ..." I felt my chest tighten and tears begin to well in my eyes. Cheryl was right. He was already regretting this.

"Please don't say it. I didn't mean what you're thinking. I don't want you to pull away, and I'm certainly not pulling away on my end at all. I just meant this is special. You don't see this in life often. This is kismet." He gestured between us.

I heard his words answer the fears in my head, almost as though he were reading my thoughts again; yet the tears still came. I had no idea why. I just suddenly felt relieved. In fact, I felt great relief at hearing him dispel the worries that had been planted in my head earlier that morning. He reached up and wiped a tear away and then put it to his lips. It was a very sweet gesture. He pulled me closer to him and cupped my cheek.

"Sydney, I have waited my whole life to meet a girl like you. Actually, I think I was waiting to meet you. Now we have this *one chance* to have something other people search for their whole lives. It's being handed to us. I don't want to stop or slow down. I want to be with you. Why are you crying? Is this all too much?"

"I want this to be real and don't want to lose you. I don't want this to end, and it's barely even started."

"I have no intentions of leaving you. If it ends, it will be because you chose something else, a different ending to your story."

"To my fairytale?" I'm not sure why I used the same words from my conversation with Cheryl, but maybe it was because he played off them by using the word 'story.' They just seemed to fit. But this was more than a simple fairytale or story; this *was* real.

"Yes, if you want to call it that. But not every fairytale has a happy ending, Sydney. It's all about how it's perceived. Don't you agree? Some people think happiness is all about having money and fancy things. While others find happiness in a trailer park, barely making it by. It's all in their perception. Happiness is a matter of perception."

"So, it's what I perceive as making me happy?"

"Yes. What you perceive as your fairytale happy ending, someone else might not think is the right ending at all, or a happy ending at that. Does that make any sense?"

"It makes perfect sense to me. Right now, being with you ... it makes me happier than I've ever been." I thought about Cheryl's perception of Aiden verses mine.

"So you think being with me could be your happy ending?" He waited for my response with an adorable smile.

"It's certainly looking that way. I've just never connected to someone like this ever before. We click."

"We do click." He tousled my hair, released me and began to get out of bed.

"I'm going to get ready for our day. Would you like to use the bathroom first?" I wanted to share the bathroom with him this morning. Visions of showering with him dominated my head.

"I won't be too long. There's a fresh pot of coffee downstairs. Bet I'll be finished before you get back up here." *Oh, I'd be finished all right.* My plan was to get myself off in the shower because he had me so turned on right now. Just his body pressed against mine was enough to do the trick. This man had a very strange effect on me. I considered taking an extra long shower so he would have time to get his coffee and join me. I smiled at myself and proceeded to do my thing.

I wanted to look nice, but still remain casual. This was our first date and I wanted to look pretty for him. I applied my signature light make-up, straightened my hair, and wondered if he'd like it this way. I chose a pair of skinny jeans, thumbhole shirt, and a cute jacket shirt with a fleece lining. I wanted to be warm, but not too warm because I needed him to come to the rescue of the freezing damsel in distress with his hot body.

We reconvened downstairs in the kitchen.

I grabbed cold cuts and began making various finger sandwich scenarios so we had a few different options. Aiden diced cheese, then made wine suggestions from my rack to compliment the assortment. We packed up the bag with lunch, stemware, and a blanket, and embarked on our date to spend the entire day at the park together.

When we got there, we looked for a spot by the river. Aiden found the most private and beautiful one that he could. I had been to this park a hundred times before and had never seen this section. It was almost like he knew exactly where it was.

We spread out our bounty and began to nosh while chatting and occasionally pawing each other.

"Do you believe in fate, Sydney?"

"Why do you ask? That's an odd question." I didn't really think it was odd; I just wanted to see where he was going with it.

"Really? Because I think it's perfect, based on how we met and the way things are progressing," he told me.

"So you believe we were *destined* to meet?"

"I completely believe with every essence of my being, that you and I were destined to be together."

"So those mythological fates are real to you?" I questioned with a hint of playfulness.

"Please don't make light of this. It's something I strongly believe in. Think about it. What are the chances we would have met in regular everyday life if it hadn't been for this war? I'm not even from this area to begin with. Had I not joined the army, I would never have been here to meet you." His toned turned quite serious.

"Where *are* you from? You haven't said much about your past. Your files don't say much, either. It didn't even list your most recent address." He now seemed uncomfortable that I was bringing work up.

"Why does it matter? I'm here with you now. Isn't that all that counts? Our pasts mean nothing. They're done and over with. They're irrelevant."

I was starting to hear Cheryl in my head again. He wouldn't even tell me where he was from. *Didn't most people like to talk about their past? Was he hiding something from me? Even worse, was he hiding from someone?*

"Are you saying the past means nothing?"

"Only the present truly exists. The past is over, and nothing can be changed or rearranged from it. The future doesn't exist yet. There's no reason to worry about it as everything is already decided. All that matters is right here and right now," he stated matter-of-factly.

"I'm not sure I agree with that. The past is what makes you who you are today. Someone might not be able to change their past, but they can certainly correct things from it, by learning from their mistakes. And the future, well you can plan for that, make it what you want it to be. Are you saying none of that matters?"

"Not exactly. I agree you can make adjustments from the past. I also believe you can think about your future and try to plan for it. But what happens ... happens. And we have no control over the consequences life throws at us. We just have to deal with it as it comes."

"I don't want to fight about this." I really didn't want to ruin our day with our first disagreement.

"Are we fighting? I thought we were just talking. I just want to know what you believe." He didn't seem upset when he said it, rather surprised instead at my thought that we were fighting. I guess he was just making conversation. I really did want to hear what his thoughts were.

"Okay. I believe in destiny to a degree. I think there's a reason you cross paths with certain people. They are meant to teach you something or bring something into your life that might not have been there on its own accord. Fate? I'm not sure about fate. I used to believe that if you weren't where you were supposed to be when you died, that's when a freak accident would happen."

"That's an interesting theory. Tell me more," he said.

"I just don't think fate decides this person will die of cancer or be paralyzed. I don't think fate says this child will be stillborn, but this one gets to live. It seems unfair. I think some things just happen, maybe for scientific reasons."

"Do you believe in God?"

"I believe in some sort of greater being. Yes, I guess if you want to say God. God is a personal experience to each individual person. I guess God is maybe one thing to me, and a different thing to someone else. What culture you were born in is also a factor that forms your personal relationship with God. I don't think God would hold it against any of us, if say, I was taught as a Catholic, versus a Buddhist being taught who God is to them. Same being, just a different perception of what God is. There's no way we could just exist. I'm pretty sure my belief process would have me excommunicated from my church. See, I think religion is very egocentric when it comes to man. Why would God create only man in his image? And why would he choose the most selfish and destructive of every living thing on earth if he were a righteous God? I believe that every living thing is created in His image." I was rambling.

"I'm enjoying your thought process on all of this. Please, go on."

"Okay, when you die, all the pieces of you that were there when you were alive are still there, the blood, bones, tissue. Except one thing is missing. That spark, the energy that made them all function. I think that's the soul. And every living thing has that same energy that makes it living until it dies, and that spark is gone."

"So energy is your soul and every living thing has a soul?" he asked me.

"Right, because that's the part of us that was created in God's image. I think heaven is a giant mass of energy. And ghosts, if they exist, are just drops of energy that never connected with the heaven mass."

"So you believe in ghosts?" He laughed and ran his hand through his hair.

"Don't make fun of me, you asked for this. Think about a residual haunting. When that person was alive, maybe they did the same routine every day. When they're dead, and if they become a ghost, that same action continues to happen over and over again. The energy keeps repeating itself because it knows nothing else. The energy is burned into time."

"Really? Sydney, that's a very interesting idea. But what if you're wrong?"

"So you don't believe in ghosts, God, or afterlife?"

"I didn't say that. I'm just not sure I agree with you. What I do believe in, as I've mentioned, is fate. Everything that happens, happens for a reason. Your path is chosen before you're even born. It explains déjà vu very nicely, don't you think?" Again he was questioning me. I wasn't sure why he was so fascinated with my thoughts on this but I was still enjoying the conversation.

"I've heard a different theory on déjà vu recently." I thought about Gina's explanation from this morning. "So what you're saying is we're aware of our destiny before we're born?"

"I like to think so. I believe everyone chooses the path they're supposed to take. I'm not saying it always goes as planned, so your freak accident scenario does coincide quite nicely there. I'm sure there are instances when something throws a monkey wrench into the whole thing and fate has to make adjustments." He spoke as though he knew this information.

"Ah, so you agree with my freak accident theory?"

"Maybe," he chuckled. He lay down on his back and looked up into the sky. "Do you ever look at the clouds?"

I was a bit confused by the complete and very random change of subject. I noticed he had modified the subject a few times already.

"Sure. I used to do it a lot as a child. I haven't lately."

"Then cloud watch with me."

I shrugged and joined him. He reached over to hold my hand as we searched for images of animals in the sky. It wasn't long before I realized I couldn't care less about the clouds, and couldn't take my eyes off him.

"Are you staring at me, Sydney?"

"Yes."

"Is something wrong?"

"No."

"Then why are you staring at me?"

"Because you're extremely hot. Plus I'm trying to send you secret telepathic messages."

"Damn, my psychic abilities are off today, unless you meant

this." He rolled onto his side and ran a fingertip across my cheek and down my neck. He leaned over and kissed me softly.

"See, that's all I've been able to think about. Is that what you were trying to send me?" he chuckled.

"It worked! How about a little more? Wait, I'll tell you with my mind." He smirked and went to town on my lips. I was happy we were in a private spot, because our actions were not appropriate for all ages.

We stayed at the park until the sun began to set and then headed home, stopping off only for more wine and take out, so we could continue our fun with no worries.

7
CHERYL

We were just about to start dinner and a movie when the phone rang. I reached over Aiden to grab it and he pulled me onto his lap.

"Hello?"

"Sydney, I'm so sorry. I'm being a total ass about this whole thing. I mean, I still think you're crazy for having a stranger in your house, but Gina has spent the entire day laying into me about how unfeeling I'm being. She keeps telling me how it was like that for us. Instant chemistry."

Cheryl didn't apologize ever. She usually was always right, too. But today was different. Either Gina was denying her sex or she really meant it.

"Cheryl, it's fine, really. You're just looking out for me. I know that, and I love you for it."

"No, that's a little too generous of you. It's seriously been bothering me all day. I must have called you a hundred times to tell you how sorry I am. There was no answer, and then that would get me going. I kept picturing you lying there murdered and in pieces." She said the last part under her breath.

"Cheryl, is this supposed to be you apologizing?"

"I know, I suck at this. I'm all over the place. I want you to be happy and have you to meet someone and fall in love. I don't want you to be alone for the rest of your life. I want you to have what I have, so I don't want to be the one holding you back from finding love. But at the same time, I don't want to see you get hurt."

"Wow, Cheryl, you're doing a fantastic job of making everything better between us."

"See? There I go again. I've been so back and forth on this all day, Gina must have whiplash by now. Don't listen to any of the messages on your voicemail, okay? Promise me."

"Okay, I'll delete them all. I forgive you."

"So we're good?"

"Of course we are. We *always* are." I heard a huge sigh of relief surge through the phone.

"Well, I still want you to be careful; you don't know this guy."

"Yeah, I think you forgot to take your meds today, you silly girl. Look, I feel like I know him. Completely. It's just so weird. It's like he's in my soul." I felt Aiden's arms tighten around me. He liked what I had said. I snuggled closer to him.

"Well, I'll have to trust your judgment on this. But I ... *we* want to meet him."

"How about Friday night? I mean, he's living here, so it's not like he'll be crashing our girls' night."

"Deal. We'll bring enough pizza for four. Is he good with pizza? Does he like it?" He could hear her and shook his head in agreement.

"He loves pizza. Sounds like the perfect plan. Talk to you later, then?"

"Bye, Sweets.

"Night, Love."

I checked my voicemail and there were no messages at all from Cheryl or anyone. I could only guess it was some sort of outage with the phone company again. I was sure they would come through later and I would delete them without listening, as promised.

8
AIDEN

"Everything okay, Syd?" Aiden said, as he played with a strand of my hair.

"Everything's fine. It's just my best friend, Cheryl. She's worried about our relationship moving too fast. She doesn't agree with your living with me, being that we just met. She thinks I'm crazy."

"Doesn't she believe in love at first sight?" I could tell immediately he regretted his choice of wording.

"Are we talking love here?" I couldn't wait to hear his response. He seemed to fidget slightly in his seat.

"I didn't mean to imply anything by that. It's just an expression."

"Oh." I averted my eyes from his, as I had been hoping for a different answer.

"You do believe in love at first sight, don't you? I certainly do," he proclaimed, his thumb on my chin, lifting my face so he could look directly into my eyes.

I felt butterflies in my stomach as my face blushed. "I didn't until I met you." I looked up at him from under my eyelashes to gauge his reaction to my words. One side of his mouth turned up in a sexy smirk. I was amazed at how every small facial expression or way he said something made me want to jump his bones. I found him irresistible.

"You have no idea how much that means to me, to hear you say that." I could almost feel the irises of my eyes dilate as I stared at his handsome face, and actually heard him confirm we were experiencing the same thing.

"Cheryl believes in love at first sight, but I don't think she understands what's happening between us. I think she's afraid you're some sort of stalker or secret murderer. She knows nothing about you."

"That's absurd. I can assure you, I'm none of those things."

"You know, I really *don't* know much about you. I've told you all about my family, friends and past, but you haven't mentioned anything at all. I brought it up at lunch, but you never answered."

"Oh, but I did. I remember saying it didn't matter anymore. My past is nothing but a shadow of who I used to be."

"Well, I'd really like to know everything about you. I want to know what your parents were like; if you have siblings. I want to know if you played sports in high school or maybe you were in marching band. Did you have a happy childhood? Were you an adorable little boy? Was your dad in the military and you're following in his footsteps? I want to know what your favorite color is. What's your favorite food?"

"So you want the whole bio? Slow down," he said with a chuckle. "Well, I can definitely say I was not in the marching band. My favorite color is blue. I like Thai food the best, but I'm a guy, so anything edible works for me."

"Well, at least I got something out of you."

"Sydney, why does it matter so much to you? Can't I just forget my past and start a new life with you? Really, all of those things, none of them matter to me; not where I came from, not who my family is. I just want to be with you." My heart quickly became a puddle in my chest. I wanted to give this man everything. I always believed that when love knocked at your door, you put your own feelings aside to give it anything the heart desired. There wasn't anything I wouldn't do to make Aiden happy, even if it included returning him to his family and possibly losing him.

"Don't you miss them? Don't you want them to know you're alive and safe? At least let them know where you are?"

"No, Sydney. No one needs to know where I am but you and me. Why are you asking me all these questions? Did your friend put doubts in your head about me?" He looked very upset, and even his voice had a quality of sadness. *Or was it panic?*

"Actually, yes, but just a smidgen. When I'm with you I don't care, because all I feel is what's between us. And believe me, it's so strong and deep. And I'm being a little bit selfish there too, because I want you all to myself. And right now, I have that. However, I've asked you things about who you are, and I get no response at all, or you just tell me it doesn't matter. We did just meet. Getting to know each other is part of the whole experience. It's part of the fun of a new relationship. It's not fair that it's so one-sided."

"Because it doesn't matter. Trust me, it really doesn't. All that matters is right here, right now."

"You keep saying that, Aiden, but I'm not buying why. I'm starting to think you're hiding something."

His face grimaced as though he was in pain, and his skin tone turned a slight hue of gray.

"Why can't you just trust me? Please," he begged.

"Because I don't know you, Aiden. I mean, I do trust you or you wouldn't be here alone in my house with me. Honestly, I just need these questions answered for work."

"Please, don't insult my intelligence. Work has nothing to do with this right now. Everything was fine until your friend starting making you over think everything."

"Maybe when she meets you on Friday, she'll change her mind.

And maybe, if you tell me some things other than benign facts, I'd feel more comfortable, too."

"I'd rather wait until you have faith in my existence with you, and then meet her. I'm not sure I make the best impression."

"What is that supposed to mean? You don't want to meet my friends? You also don't want to introduce me to anyone who knows you. Are you embarrassed of me?"

"It's nothing like that," he said sternly.

What was happening? Our wonderful day was quickly being ruined by this entire conversation. My emotions were all over the place. Getting some space between us, and fast, seemed to be the best course of action.

"I'm going to my room. I want some time alone to think. I'm pretty sure you need to do the same thing."

"Sydney, please don't go. I can't exist without you. You mean everything to me. I'm sorry." His pleas were desperate.

I didn't understand why he was acting as if this were the end of the world. I just thought we needed a break for a little while to cool down. I didn't really want to leave him, but I needed to reset myself for his sake. An emotional Sydney is not the best person to have a serious conversation with. I was all about emotions first and logic second. It was an occupational hazard. Let your emotions free; don't bottle them up. At this point, though, I certainly didn't want to blurt something out that would hurt him anymore than I probably already had. I wanted everything to go back to the lighthearted fun we'd been having.

"I'm just going to my room for a little while. You can help yourself to dinner. It's still in the kitchen. I'm not really hungry right now." I was sure my voice held no secrets to the fact I was pretty upset at the moment. I didn't want to be.

I walked up the stairs, and noticed he was following me with his head hung down like a child being sent to bed without supper. I was about to spin around to yell at him, but he walked past me, moving right to his room. It was almost eerie, as though I wasn't even there and he was only a shadow of himself. I wanted to take back everything I had said to him downstairs that made him think I doubted him. I wanted to pull him onto my bedroom and make love to him all night. My guilt was taking over my emotions, so I knew what I had to do was let him think about opening up to me. I entered my room, and listened for his door to shut.

I wasn't sure whether I wanted to cry or break something. I was furious with him for not letting me in. I was furious with Cheryl for putting all these stupid thoughts in my head in the first place. I also didn't want to lose him. I felt the wedge that existed between us right now. It was ripping into my entire being, draining everything I had. My whole reaction to this was kind of freaking me out. It felt so real and serious. *Maybe I was PMSing or something.* I threw myself on my bed and felt my tears start. Within seconds I heard a soft knocking on my door.

"Sydney? Are you crying? Please don't cry. I don't mean to cause you any pain. I can't know that I'm the cause for your tears. It's ripping my soul apart."

I ran to the door, flung it open, and fell into his arms. I desperately tried to stifle my weeping; allowing only muffled whimpers to break through. He pulled me close, holding my head against his chest, right over his heart.

"Baby, everything is going to be all right. Please just let things happen on their own. I'm not hiding my past from you. Everything will come to light in time, and you'll understand why who I was just doesn't matter to me anymore. I feel like I came back to be with you, to have something better than I had before. You're giving me that. Please don't take it away. Please don't turn away from me."

"I'm not turning away from you. I just don't want there to be any secrets. It's not the way to start a healthy relationship."

"I promise, that in time, you'll know everything there is to possibly know about me. Anything your little heart desires, you'll know. But not yet. I have to work through some things out in my own head first. You should understand; you're my case manager. Isn't this normal?"

"There is no normal for soldiers returning. Every case is different. I'm sorry. I should've considered that as an option. You're *not* ready, are you?" I was approaching epic fail status as his case manager. I wasn't thinking straight, not for any aspect of my life. *What was wrong with me?* I really felt terrible.

"No, not yet. I promise you. I won't break that, not to you. Is that okay? "

"I'm a complete idiot." I wasn't really thrilled with his answer, but he was right. I was completely neglecting the fact that he had almost died. That alone had to have a huge impact on how he felt about life and not what existed before he met me. I was almost ashamed of myself.

"No, you're not, not at all. You're entitled to want to know who's living with you. Let's not let it ruin our entire day. It's been wonderful and I just want it to continue. Please don't feel badly. "

"I'll try?" I squeaked out. It wasn't convincing at all.

"How about a little smile for me? I'll wrestle you if you don't." He looked like he was going to pounce on me, so I gave him an all-teeth-grin, which probably made me look like I was in pain.

"I'll take it. But I still might have at you for some fun," he said.

We headed downstairs, hand in hand. Dinner was not as lively as our day in the park had been. We were mostly quiet, occasionally sharing a smile with each other over forkfuls of food. I wasn't sure if he was afraid to say anything so as not to start another fight. Maybe it was only because we were watching a movie during dinner. I would look up at him, only to always find him watching me, as though if he took his eyes off me, I might disappear.

Aiden fell asleep somewhere around ten, halfway through the movie. I couldn't keep myself from watching him this time. I had to keep checking to make sure he was really here with me. Maybe I was afraid if I took *my* eyes off *him, he'd* disappear. He was just so peaceful. I cleaned up dinner, and then woke him.

"Hey, sleepyhead, why don't you head on up? I'm going to finish watching the movie. You can stay here with me, if you want."

"Oh, did I fall asleep? It's so easy to rest when you're next to me. You're so comfortable and warm. Plus, I don't have any nightmares when you're beside me. I think I'll go on up. I'll see you in the morning."

"Wake me if you get up before me so I can make coffee and breakfast."

"I will." He kissed me gently on the top of my head and ran his hand down my cheek. I watched his sexy ass walk up the stairs. *God, this man was really just too hot.* I thought about following him, but then thought better about it. I didn't want our relationship based on only desire, especially after we had our first disagreement today.

After the movie was over, I shut everything down and moved upstairs to bed. I threw on a cami and a pair of boy short panties, and headed to the bathroom to brush my teeth. I could hear small whimpers coming from Aiden's room. I checked the door, and it was unlocked, so I went in.

He was lying in bed, tossing and turning, making small noises that I could tell were not pleasant ones. He seemed extremely distressed. I crawled into bed to spoon him. I couldn't help myself. As soon as I was next to him, I heard him let out a long, soft sigh, and he was back to restful sleep. Sleeping next to him made me feel safe and comfortable, too. Everything about him made me feel that way. I hadn't realized how nervous I had been all this time living here alone. I also needed to be close to him. The fights we had during today had drained me emotionally. Not sleeping beside him was quickly becoming something I could not live without.

When light filtered into the room in the morning, I felt his fingers run down my arm. I stirred slightly, but he was so warm and cozy that I didn't want to move. I gave him a slight smile, and then drifted back into semi-consciousness. His fingertips soon transformed into his lips, and he was running them up and down my arm. I could feel goose bumps starting to rise, along with a sweet ache forming between my legs. I turned toward him and started to kiss his chest and neck.

He responded quickly by flipping me onto my back, and then rolling on top of me. Soon our lips were locked in a passionate kiss. Our hands began to wander everywhere. I was becoming increasingly hot for him, every touch, and every kiss overflowing with extreme desire for this man. His breath became ragged and his eyes were heavy with lust.

"Sydney, I can barely hold back. We need to stop or this is going to get to a point where I won't be able to. I want you so badly. You have no idea."

"Yes, I do. Right there with you." Yet I continued to paw, nibble, and kiss.

He took my hands, brought them above my head, held them there and stared deeply into my eyes.

"I want you, Sydney, more than you can even imagine. But I want all of you, your body, your heart, and your soul. Do you understand?"

His eyes bored into me. I felt like he was melting into me, as though we were connecting on some strange cellular level. My hips involuntarily started to grind into his. My body started to hum and tingle all over. His body responded in kind, and soon we were going through all the tender motions of making love but still in our clothing.

I was aching for him so badly, but he continued to hold my arms captive above my head. I wanted to run my hands over every inch of him. It was almost torturous to be held back. As if he could read my thoughts, a deep groan escaped his lips and he relinquished his grip on them. Aiden hovered above me, running his eyes over my body and face.

"You're so beautiful, Sydney. I need to feel you against me. Please." I nodded, and he was back on top of me. The feel of him was too much. I couldn't take it. Apparently he couldn't, either. Our tenderness turned toward intense passion. It was only a matter of time before I wouldn't be able to keep myself from jumping out of my clothes and then aggressively jumping him.

"Sydney, we have to stop. I'm not ready for this to happen."

Was he kidding me? He wanted to stop now? I wanted to keep going. In fact, I was ready to go all the way. He kissed me gently and started to move away from me.

"No, don't go, not yet. Hold me like this for a while, please. Don't ever let me go."

He gave me a sultry smile and pressed his body back against mine. I wished we were completely undressed, so I could have every inch of my skin touching his, but I knew that would be the end of slowing things down. I made no requests of him. He rubbed his body over mine, the feel of it sending shivers throughout me. I hugged him so tightly, hoping to pull his soul inside. The hum I always felt when we touched seemed to softly vibrate my entire being. I was getting too aroused again, so I began to take deep breaths to slow myself.

"You're not going to hyperventilate, are you?"

"No, silly. I'm just trying to calm myself down. Tell me you're not having the same problem?"

"Oh, I'm definitely having a similar experience to yours. I'm sorry I'm holding us back. I just want this to happen at the right time."

"This isn't the right time?"

"Not yet. But I'm hoping it will be soon."

"Well, that's very cryptic of you."

"Good things come to those that wait. It won't be long, I can tell you that, based on how hard it is to stop today."

"I'm all yours, just say the word." I didn't care anymore. Being like this with him, everything was pure bliss. All the issues from yesterday seemed to have melted away at his touch.

9
CHERYL

I needed to head into the office, at least for a little while, to check my desk. It had been a few days, and although I had logged into my email, I wanted to make sure there were no new cases sitting in my bin. I was having small panic attacks and doubting that I had actually read the note that had been left on my desk correctly, second-guessing not having to be at work. The government was notorious for saying one thing, but doing something completely different. It was all about the red tape.

I hated the thought of leaving Aiden. He withdrew when I told him my plan. He seemed to exhibit slight depression, and was obviously having a bit of separation anxiety. *This was why I had never gotten a cat.* I felt so guilty, and honestly, I didn't want to leave him, either. He clung to me like it was the last time we would see each other. I assured him I wouldn't be gone long, and kissed him deeply so he would know I meant it. He watched out the window as I drove away.

I didn't even remember driving to work, it seemed automated. I tried to recall if I had run any red lights on the way here as I had been lost in my thoughts about Aiden. I parked in my regular spot, and continued over to security to sign in.

"Good morning, Ma'am. ID please," a young, pleasant-looking officer addressed me.

"Here you go. Where's Harry? Did he finally take that dream vacation he was always talking about?"

"I'm sorry to tell you this, Ms. Porter, but Harry passed away." My heart sank in my chest. I tried to maintain my composure.

"Oh my God! When? What happened? I just spoke to him the other day." I was truly heartbroken.

"Two days ago, Ma'am. I'm not sure of the exact circumstances. Sorry for your loss."

I took my ID and shook my head in disbelief. He was one of the healthiest people I knew. He must have died the last day I had seen him. I would have to find out from Cheryl about his funeral arrangements. I was surprised she hadn't mentioned it to me on the phone. She knew that I had a sweet spot in my heart for him.

I did a quick drive-by my office, only to find a film of dust waiting for me. I guess I really had nothing to worry about. I turned direction and veered straight down to see Cheryl.

She was sitting at her desk with her back to me, so I decided a sneak attack was in order. I tiptoed up behind her and right as I was about to put my hands over her eyes, she swung her chair around to face me.

"Well, hello there, Lazarus. Came to join the living at work today?" she mused sarcastically.

"Ha. Ha. Very funny, but I think you meant the Prodigal Son."

"Whatever. What forces have allowed you to grace our presence this fine day?" I could already see her sarcasm was here to stay.

"I was nervous. I'm not used to working from home. I needed to come in and check my desk to calm my fears."

"Oh, I hear ya there."

"So, how come you didn't tell me about Harry?" I was actually quite upset that she hadn't even considered calling me with the news. She knew how much I enjoyed seeing him every morning. We even had an ongoing joke about my running away with him someday.

"I'm sorry, honey. It completely slipped my mind. Occupational hazard, you know?"

"Okay. It's just, I hope I didn't miss his funeral." For me, the funeral was all about saying goodbye. They're the best way to bring closure. Something about crying at a wake with the family and friends, then going to the cemetery, it just brought it all home for me. Every time I missed a funeral, it just felt open-ended, like I was waiting for something, just not sure what.

"There's a message on the board about it. You can check it out before you leave. Can you stay for lunch? I'm meeting Gina at the diner. I know she'd love to see you."

"Oh, I don't know. Aiden looked pretty upset that I left today. I should really get back to him."

"Sydney, what's going on? Did this guy take over your life? First you decide that you don't have to come into the office anymore. Now you have no time to spend with your friends. What's going to happen when his case is over and everything goes back to normal?"

"What the hell is that supposed to mean? There's nothing going on. I just like being with him. And who says everything is going to go back to normal?"

"So you don't like being with anyone else? Life can't just end because of Aiden, you know."

"It's not. You're being ridiculous."

"It's just that I did a little research."

"I'm not liking this already, Cher. What did you do?"

"Okay, I'll tell you, but promise not to get mad. I looked at incoming and couldn't find anyone with the name Aiden."

"Because he's highly classified, Cheryl. I told you that. You need special clearance. Are we going to get into this again?" I shook my head and looked down at the floor.

"Nope. I'm done. I can tell you don't want to discuss this anymore and neither do I. I've said what I had to, and anyway, Gina told me to zip my lips. Well, at least when it comes to Aiden. Otherwise, she likes my lips all unzipped."

"Too much information, Cher." I put my fingers in my ears and made a *la la la* noise. We were suddenly back at ease and giggling together. It was always that way for us. One simple joke and all tension went out the door.

"Please, won't you come to lunch with us? I have something else I want to talk to you about."

"Is it good news?" I really needed some right now.

"I should let Gina tell you. She'll kick my ass if I ruin her surprise."

"A surprise? Can't you give me a little hint?" I held my fingers up and showed her how little her hint should be.

"No!"

"Fine. I'll go call Aiden and let him know I'll be running late. Does that satisfy you?"

"Not as much as Gina does, but it sounds like a plan, babe. I'm really happy you're coming. I feel like I never see you anymore. I don't like it. I miss you too much. Meet you back down here in a little while?"

I shook my head as I walked away. It had only been a few days since I had been with Aiden. She was acting like it had been months without seeing me.

10

AIDEN

I headed back to my office for some privacy. I dialed my home number, hoping Aiden would pick up.

"Hello, Sydney. Is everything okay? I didn't expect to hear from you until you got back."

"Hey, babe. I'm so glad you felt comfortable enough to answer my phone. I was hoping you would. Everything's just fine. Well, actually, not completely fine."

"What's wrong? What happened?" He sounded truly worried, on the verge of panic even.

"I just found out a friend of mine died." I could feel the tears welling in my eyes.

"Oh, I'm so sorry. Was it unexpected?" His voice was filled with concern and compassion now.

"I guess so. I don't know. Harry was always so full of life, happy, and healthy. I mean, he was an older gentleman, but seemed to be in great shape for his age. It's just so sad that he's not in my life anymore."

"Death isn't final, you know," he said softly.

"It sure feels final. I didn't even get to say goodbye."

"Death is just another chapter in our existence, Sydney. I'm sure he knows you're grieving for him. I like to think that the dead are just on another level of consciousness. They can still hear the thoughts of their loved ones or those around them, until they choose to shut them off and move on."

"That's a comforting way of thinking about it. If I died and could still be with my loved ones, I'd never move on." I thought about his words in regards to my parents. For a few months after they passed, I felt their presence all around me. They seemed to have moved on after I was settled in the house and felt resolution and closure about what had happened to them. I woke up one morning and never felt them around me again.

He mumbled something under his breath. I hadn't been completely focused on him and had missed it.

"What did you say?" I questioned.

"Oh nothing. So are you leaving soon to come home? I miss you. I miss every single breath you take."

"That's so sweet. I miss you, too. I won't be home right away. I just wanted to let you know I'm going to be running a bit behind. I'm going to catch lunch with Cheryl and Gina. I haven't seen them for a few days."

"Are you sure that's wise? We're running out of time."

"Running out of time? I'm not sure I understand what you mean by that." It took all my strength to keep Cheryl's voice out of my head.

"I meant for nice weather. Sorry I didn't finish my thought there. Sometimes I just assume you're in my head thinking the same things I am *with me*. It usually seems to be that way with us. I like that. Anyway, we're supposedly getting a bad ice storm later this week. I thought we could go for a walk in the woods together today before the weather turns. But if you're going to run late, we won't have enough light when you get back."

"Can we go tomorrow morning? I was actually thinking of

asking you if you wanted to go jogging with me. I haven't gone since you've been staying with me and I'm feeling it."

"I'm not sure it's wise for me to go jogging just quite yet."

"Right, sorry. I forgot since you won't talk to me about anything yet."

"Sydney, we talked about that last night. Please let's not go through this all again."

"Fine, but at least you could give me important medical information, so I'm not asking you to do stupid things."

"Don't be silly. I'm healthy, I just hate jogging. It's been awhile, as you can imagine. I just thought you might not question me and let me get away with using it as an excuse." He chuckled.

"Oh, I see your evil plan. So, you're cool with me going to lunch?"

"I really wish you wouldn't. I'd feel more comfortable knowing you're here with me. But if you have to, I guess I don't have a choice. Do I?"

"Why are you being like this?" I was thoroughly annoyed with both him and Cheryl right now and thought about ditching them both, and only going to lunch with Gina.

"Like what?" he responded innocently.

"Difficult. You're all over the place lately."

"Are you having doubts? And are they *your* doubts or someone else's?"

"That's not fair, Aiden. I'm not doubting you," I reassured him.

"I just know if you go, your friend is going to start making you question things again."

"Cheryl is my best friend and I've known her forever, a heck of a lot longer than I've known you. She just points out things I might be missing because I'm on cloud nine when it comes to us. Sometimes she just opens my eyes and helps me work things out in my head."

"Sometimes you need to make choices of your own accord."

"This isn't about making choices. I choose you both." It was the truth. I didn't have to choose one over the other. I wanted them both in my life.

"What if you can't have both of us?"

What the hell is happening here? I had no idea how this phone call had gone so terribly wrong. The quick frequency of our recent arguments was starting to wear on my mind.

"Look, you have nothing to worry about. I'll be home before you know it. Time will fly by."

"Yes. Time does pass before us very quickly and then it's gone."

"Oh so serious. Stop, babe. It's just lunch." I almost told him I loved him, but managed to get control of my mouth for once. It just seemed like I was supposed to say it. It felt right.

"All right, Syd, but remember, I'm here waiting for you."

"How could I forget? You're always on my mind. What will you be wearing when I get home?" I flirted with him, hoping to rebalance our conversation to a happier one.

"Maybe nothing but a smile. You'll have to hurry to find out."

"Noted."

"I miss you, Sydney."

"That's a good thing, Aiden. The feeling is *very* mutual. I'll be in your arms before you know it. Bye."

11
CHERYL

Gina was waiting outside the diner for us, looking adorable as ever in her black dance pants, pink leggings, and an off-the-shoulder pink sweatshirt. She kissed Cheryl and gave me her winning smile as they walked arm in arm into the diner. I used to be jealous of the love they had, but now I had found my own. I thought about Aiden and realized how lucky I actually was. It was like he had just fallen out of heaven and answered all of my prayers.

"So, tell me. What's the good word, G?" I noticed she shot Cheryl a dirty look as soon as the words left my mouth.

"I told her nothing. You said not to speak of it, so I didn't. I know what's dangerous to my health and sex life."

"Good girl. Okay, well, I kind of lied to you the other day, Sydney. We found a donor a little over a month and a half ago. We didn't want to jinx it until we knew he was on board."

"Oh my God, I'm so excited for you. So when are you going to do the nasty with him?"

"Really, Syd? You know that's not how it's done," Cheryl was speaking with pure jealousy at that point. No other woman, and for that matter, no man, was ever going to touch Gina in any way.

"I kid. I kid. Give me all the deets." I held my hands up in submission.

I watched as Cheryl took Gina's hand in hers and they shared a loving glance. Again, instead of pangs of jealousy, I felt bliss.

"It's already done."

"What's already done? You already got the okay from him?"

"No, we're pregnant. It's really early and I shouldn't be telling anyone yet, but you're family."

I literally flew over the table and grabbed them both into a huge hug. I was overcome with complete happiness at the thought of a new life coming into this world, their world. Our world. It made the loss of Harry today seem not as somber. One life left this world as another was entering it. It seemed so simple.

"Oh my God! I don't even know what to say. Congratulations! This is so amazing." All three of us had tears in our eyes.

"I think she's more excited than you were, Cher."

"That's because I'm scared out of my mind. I deal with death all day. This is out of my domain."

"You're going to be a great mom. A great dad? Which one are you again?" I giggled.

"You're very cute, Syd. Or should I say, Auntie Nini?"

I was going to be an aunt. I was having a hard time comprehending it all. I thought about if Aiden and I had children. *Wow, I was actually thinking about having a child with Aiden?* I wanted everything with him, a fulfilling life with all the bells and whistles. Hearing this news drove that home. It put everything into perspective. This had to be the true meaning of life.

They filled me in on all the details about the father and why they had chosen him. He resembled Cheryl in appearance, which was very important to them both, since the baby would actually be Gina's flesh and blood. Gina told me how they could've passed for siblings.

The man was extremely intelligent, having a degree from Harvard in biology, and worked in pharmaceutical research. But most importantly, he was willing to father the child and be only an observer in raising the baby. They wanted to give their child the opportunity to know him, should he or she ever so choose, and also allow the donor to see the child growing up without any worries of him trying to reclaim it.

They said he was a very kind man, who was heavily involved in fundraising work for cancer patients, having lost his wife to breast cancer. They had never had any children of their own before she died, but had wanted them dearly. He had told them his wife would have been thrilled he was doing this wonderful thing for them. He knew he would never marry again, as she had been his soul mate and the only woman for him. They had bonded over that, and knew he was the right man for the job. He had even turned down any payment for his services. He had donated in honor of his wife's memory.

I heard about due dates and doctor's appointments, and how they were going to decorate the nursery. They even invited me to the first sonogram.

I loved every second of our conversation. When we finally parted ways, I couldn't wait to get home to tell Aiden everything. Again, thoughts of having a child with him were mulling through my brain. The desire to make love to him was growing exponentially greater, but wanting to bear his children made it more intense. I guess my biological clock was ticking louder than I thought.

12

AIDEN

I rushed through the front door calling for him. I heard some movement upstairs, and literally flew up two steps at a time to get to him. I opened his door, but he wasn't there. I peered around the corner to see if he was in the bathroom, but the light was off. A knot began to form in my stomach. *What if he had left? Could he possibly have taken my absence as an opportunity to leave without having to tell me why?*

"Hey, I'm glad you're home." I nearly jumped out of my skin at the sound of his soft voice behind me, where he had suddenly just materialized. I had no idea where he came from, he had just *appeared*. I heard no footsteps coming up the stairs. It was rather creepy how quietly he moved. I was sure he was a covert mission op —he moved like a ninja about my house. I wondered if he had come from my room. *What would he have been doing there in the first place?*

"You startled me."

"I didn't mean to. Let me make it better." He pulled me to him and placed a long deep kiss on my lips. Shivers of pleasure shot through me. I wanted more, but he released me.

"Yeah, that made it all better. I'd like some more, please." Even I could hear how sultry my voice sounded with that one.

"That can definitely be arranged." Now his voice was dripping with sexual overtones, too.

"Well, what's stopping you?"

His hands were on me before I knew what was happening. He swept me off my feet and pushed me quickly onto his bed. I couldn't keep from running my hands all over his body. His moved slower over mine, like a blind man trying to see every detail with his fingertips. It was as if he was studying every curve. I ran my tongue slowly over his neck, stopping only to taste him with a nibble. His breath quickened and he let out a soft breath with each bite.

It wasn't but a moment before I could no longer hold back. I wrapped my legs around his waist so he couldn't escape this time, and began to grind myself against him.

"You're going to be the death of me," he mused.

"I don't want to kill you, Baby, my plan is to show you what heaven feels like."

"Sydney," he growled as he crushed his mouth over mine. Our kisses became more frenzied.

"Everywhere you touch me, every move you're making, it's driving me insane, Aiden. I've never felt anything like this before."

He pulled me tight against him and whispered in my ear, "I love you, Sydney." My heart seized in my chest.

"Wait. What did you say?"

He pulled slowly back from me, so we were face to face. He looked deeply into my eyes and caressed my cheek.

"I said I love you, Sydney. Never have I felt so deeply for someone. I've waited for what feels like an eternity to find you. I think it has always been you I was holding out for. It's like I knew we were supposed to be together."

I wasn't sure how to respond. I knew deep inside my soul I was falling for this man. I had wanted to tell him I loved him earlier, but hearing him actually say it out loud suddenly made me nervous.

Everything was happening so fast. He was living with me already, and we had only just met. I had actually, only moments before, been thinking of having his child. The words should have come easily to me. I wanted to say them. I wanted him to hear them. I just couldn't bring myself to utter them to his waiting ears. I realized I just wasn't ready yet. Especially with our recent disagreements thrown into the mix. My mouth hung open. I tried to kiss him but he pulled away.

"Sydney, you're not feeling the same way. You don't love me." His face was suddenly tortured, as though I had ripped his heart right out of his chest.

"Aiden, it's not that I'm not feeling something so insanely far-reaching within my soul for you. I am. I can tell you that with more confidence than you could imagine. When I say those words to someone, to you, there's no turning back. It has to be forever."

"You don't see forever with me?"

"I've thought about it. I've been thinking about it every single second since I met you. But those words, when I say them, I need to be one hundred percent sure. I want to know this is going to last. Those words are final. I don't want to hurt you."

"You have no concept of how true what you're expressing is. They are final. For me, they have never been uttered to another woman before you."

"You ... you've never told anyone else you loved them? You've never *loved anyone* before?" His statement made me realize I was right in my decision not to respond in kind.

"No, Sydney. Not like this. *You* are my entire reason for existing at this very moment in time."

His words. *What was I doing?* This man just returned from war, and I had scooped him up and brought him into my own little world where he existed only for me. *How could I have done this?* I had completely failed him. I was supposed to help him get his life back. Instead I stole it for my own. I pushed him off of me and scrambled to my feet.

"Sydney, where are you going? What are you doing?" He was panicking.

"I think you need to go. I think I've made a huge mistake."

"Please. Don't say that. You have no idea the effect your words will have on me. Please, Sydney, don't do this," he begged.

"I'll call Cheryl. I'll get her friend Joe's address. You'll be better off there. We can still see each other, but we'll take things slower. I don't want you gone from my life. It's just that we fell into this relationship. It was forced. We both pushed what we have right now, and that's not what you need. You don't need me. You need to live your life and if I'm meant to be a part of it, then so be it."

"Sydney, no. Please, Baby. I haven't forced my feelings for you. I fell in love with you the moment I met you. I can't *live* without *you*."

"You just said it. You said you exist only for me right at this very moment in time. But you need to exist for yourself or what we have between us will never survive. I can't only have this moment in time. I'd fall apart if you ever changed your mind or took those words back. It really has to be forever for me, too. "

"And it does for me, too. It is already. My forever only exists if you're part of it."

"No. You're just lost. You need to find your way first. Aiden, please, this is the best thing for you. I'm going to go call a cab." It killed me inside to push him away. It tore my very soul apart. I knew I was doing the best thing for him. He deserved it. He needed someone to do the right thing and look out for his wellbeing. That was my job and I had ignored every rule I put into place to help every other soldier returning.

"If you don't want me here, I'll leave. I would never go against your wishes. I'll get my own ride. Sydney. But can I ask you one thing? Am I not worthy of your love?"

I couldn't answer him. I was the unworthy one. The light left his eyes as I watched them fill with tears. He reached his hand out for me; I turned my back to him and left the room with my hand covering my mouth to stifle my soon-to-be blubbering. I couldn't bear the thought of seeing him, or I wouldn't let him leave. Not ever. I ran to my room, locked the door behind me and bawled my little eyes out as quietly as I could.

My heart hurt. *Did I just make a huge mistake?* We weren't fighting. We were probably about to make love. I jumped up and ran to the bathroom to stop him. I didn't want him to leave me. *What had I been thinking?*

I wanted him to have the best possible opportunities to acclimate back into life. I stopped, only to slump myself against the door and listen. I could hear his muffled cries through the bathroom door. It tore yet another piece of my heart out. It was heartbreaking to hear a man cry, and even more so to hear Aiden, because I knew how much I had just hurt him.

I wasn't sure how long I had been listening to him, but soon I heard his footsteps walk down the hall to the stairs. *Strange.* It was probably one of the only times I heard him move about the house. Each step felt as though someone was plunging a dagger deeper into my heart. I tried to keep myself from running after him. But I had made this decision and had to stick with it. It was what was best for him. Maybe it was best for the both of us. When I finally heard the front door shut, the pain I already felt was unbearable.

Without actually realizing what I was doing, I pulled myself up and barreled down the hallway. I knew he couldn't have gotten very far. I hadn't even offered to drive him myself, only a ride in a cab from a stranger to take him to a place I didn't even know myself. How cruel of me. There was no way it had gotten here already. *What was wrong with me?* I was pushing the best thing that ever happened to me out of my life.

I commanded every muscle in my body to push to the limit and, surprisingly did not crash down the stairs at my extreme pace. The door flung open and I rushed outside. There was no sight of him. He must have walked to the edge of the driveway to wait for his ride. I sprinted there as quickly as possible. I was out of breath, but forcing myself to move faster before I lost him, possibly forever

There was no one standing at the edge of my driveway. No cab could be seen. He had simply vanished.

I sank down to my knees, staring into the darkness, hyperventilating. The severity of what had just transpired jolted my entire being. I didn't move for some time, hoping he would return to me. *How could he just leave?* He didn't even try to stay with me or talk me out of my decision. It was as if my will was all that existed. *How was I going to move forward without him? What had I done?*

13

SYDNEY

All I wanted to do was to curl up into fetal position, cry, and wait for him. I thought about screaming out his name, but only my neighbors and possibly all the dogs within a ten-mile radius would hear me. After mustering all my strength, I finally was able to pull myself to my feet. It took everything I had. I trudged back towards my house. The closer I got, the emptier it seemed. It was now only a hollow house, void of anything but emptiness. That was also a perfect description of what I felt in the cavity of my chest right now. I was afraid my heart no longer existed.

The house was so silent as I stepped through the doorway, almost like walking into a cemetery in the middle of the night. He was gone. I had thrown him away. *What had I done? What had I done?* I could only repeat the words over and over in my head.

I found it hard to breathe. I was suffocating in my own desperation. He hadn't been gone for more than an hour and it was already unendurable. *How was I going to survive this?*

I lay down, sobbing uncontrollably on and off for the entire night. I never left the couch except to search for some little part of him he might have left behind. I even tried smelling the throw pillows that surrounded me, just to experience his scent. But there was nothing left. He was gone, along with every single trace, as though he had never existed. His absence burned through my entire body. He was truly gone.

Even the slightest noise prompted me to jump to my feet to run to the window and check to see if he had returned. After the tenth time, I realized he wasn't coming back. Maybe he was giving me space for the night to think everything over. I'm sure he would call me in the morning. If I didn't hear from him first, I would call him. *Hell, I wanted to hear his voice now.* I wanted to hear his voice so badly I could taste it. I wanted to tell him how I thought I made a mistake. How I *knew* I had made a huge mistake. I was going to call him and tell him so. Tell him to come back to me.

I rummaged through everything on the top of my desk to locate his paperwork. I thumbed through looking for any contact number I could find. There was nothing there. *Oh my God, I had no way to reach him.* There were no family or friends listed with whom to leave a message. There was no address, email or mobile number. I had lost complete contact with him. I could only hope and pray for him to come back to me. The futility of my search brought a whole new level of darkness to my world.

No sleep came to me that evening. I spent the entire time standing vigil, waiting for his return. Staring at the window for a light to let me know he was here with me. There were a few moments I swear I felt him touch my shoulder or caress my cheek. The house seemed so cold without his presence. Again I was reminded of a cemetery. It all felt so final.

The weather had changed drastically. I could hear the rain pelting the roof and windows. I could feel the cold dampness through my clothing right to my skin. I shivered, but made no move to grab a blanket. I wanted to suffer. I needed to pay for what I had done to Aiden and to myself. It was all my own self-doing. I had ruined everything. I'm sure God would let me stay in the hell I had created for the rest of my life. I sunk deeper and deeper into darkness.

"Well, you totally fucked up, Sydney. I see you're talking to yourself now. Know why that is? Because you just ensured you'll always be alone. You sealed your own fate with this one. There's no one to listen to your pitiful ramblings anymore. You sent him away. Not only was Aiden hot as all fuck, but he loved you. He told you he loved you and what was your response? You looked away and turned your back on him. How cruel can you be, Sydney? You made a soldier cry. I don't even want to be with you right now. I wish I could make you leave and bring Aiden back. You will be alone forever. Hope you can deal with that."

Yep, there it was. I was going to be old, crazy spinster Auntie Nini, who sat in her lonely empty house talking to herself. I bet Gina and Cheryl wouldn't even want me near their children if they knew who I really was.

I knew that being sleep deprived was really not helping my disposition much. I needed to get out of this house. I didn't want to be alone right now. I needed to go see the girls. They were all I had left in this world. I could only hope they would have me.

14

CHERYL

I stood in front of the door to their apartment, wondering if it was too late or too early to knock. I felt as though I was being pushed towards the door and it was creeping me out, so I finally mustered enough strength to knock on it. Within seconds, Cheryl was standing in front of me.

"Are you all right? You look like shit! Have you been crying? Do you have any idea what time it is?" She threw it all at me in one breath, arms crossed over her chest, looking like I had woken her out of a deep sleep.

"I'm sorry. I'm a complete failure at everything I do."

"Oh, babe, you need to get in here right now. I'm going to go wake Gina." She recognized the urgency of my visit.

"No, let her rest. She's with child," I told her sternly.

"She's only a month, she'll be fine. I think this is more up her alley, don't you? Sad, sobbing friends at the door at ungodly hours... so up her alley."

"No, please. I need *you* right now."

"Me? Why? What happened? Did the soldier boy leave you? I knew it was only a matter of time."

"Yes. Aiden and I are over."

"Did he hurt you? Did you get into a fight?" she quizzed.

"No, he didn't hurt me and we didn't get in a fight. He told me he loved me."

"Are you kidding me? So you broke up with your less-than-a-week-long boyfriend because he told you he loved you? Is he at your house right now?" Her tone of voice was incredulous.

"No, I threw him out."

"You told him to leave because he loves you? Did you say it back?" Now Cheryl sounded like Gina.

"No."

"You seemed so happy with him. I know that's not the advice I gave you. I told you to take it slow. I didn't mean so slow you brought it to a screeching halt."

I didn't respond.

"I'm not sure I understand why you ended things. Tell me, it will make you feel better to say it out loud," Cheryl coaxed.

"I failed him."

"How did you fail him? You gave him a place to stay and all your attention, not to mention your affection."

"It was selfish what I did. I didn't help him. I made him my own personal case. I made him mine," I explained.

"No, honey, you didn't make him do that, he wanted to do that. It was his choice to get involved with you. He didn't have to."

"What if he felt obligated because I gave him a place to stay?" I said.

"Do you honestly believe that or do you believe he had real feelings for you?"

"I don't know what to think anymore. I just know I failed him. I was supposed to help him first, not lure him into my bed."

"And did you lure him into your bed?" she questioned.

"We never got that far."

"Well, I guess that would have complicated this even more if you'd had sex with him."

"I made a huge mistake! I miss him so much already. I hurt him so badly."

"Then call him up and tell him you're sorry. I'm sure if you just tell him how you're feeling he'll come back to at least talk things over."

"I can't," I whined.

"Why the hell not?" Cheryl just couldn't seem to comprehend how grave the situation was.

"I have no contact information on him. No phone. No previous addresses. No family or friends. No anything. It's like he never existed."

"I have something to say about all that, Syd, and you know it. But since it seems as though your heart has taken enough beating today, I'm going to bite my tongue."

"Thanks. But I deserve to have someone lash out at me."

"I'm not going to bitch at you, honey. You should know better than that. Listen, you probably already know I think you made the right decision. Just because you told him to leave your house, doesn't mean he has to leave your life, right? This will give you both a chance to move at a slower pace and make sure the feelings you have for one another are real."

"I hurt him. I might as well have just spit in his face. If I were him, I'd never come back." I sulked.

"I'm sure it's not as bad as it seems. Why don't you stay here tonight, huh? Or at least what's left of it. You need to get some rest. I bet after a good night's rest, tomorrow you'll have a whole new outlook and things won't seem as dismal. And anyway, I'm feeling cautious about letting you drive. You have deep circles under your eyes. You look like you're strung out, and I'm afraid you'll fall asleep while driving home," she said, her concern showing.

"No chance of me falling asleep at the wheel because I don't think I can sleep at all. What if he calls? I won't be there. I need to be there if he calls me. What if he thinks I'm just not answering the phone or the door, trying to avoid him? He'll leave for good then. No, I need to go home."

I could hear the panic in my voice, so I was sure Cheryl was starting to worry about my present mental condition. I put my hands over my face and began to sob. She put her hand on my shoulder to comfort me. I knew she felt terrible for me, and this was her best effort at comforting me. She was right about Gina being the one to run to.

"You need to chill, babe. I'm going to see if Gina has anything to help you relax. She can't take any of it anymore, so it might as well do someone some good."

"Please, don't leave me, Cher," I cried, as I grabbed her arm and held on for dear life.

"I'm only going to the next room, Sydney. There's only one doorway and its right there in front of you, so no sneaking out on you. I promise. I'm just not sure if I should bring you something to knock you out, space you out, or get you drunk. Maybe drunk isn't the right way to go here. You're an emotional drunk to begin with, especially when you're in a mood, and this is definitely one those moods."

"I don't want anything. I need to feel the rawness of the pain, so I know how I made him feel tonight. I deserve to feel like the piece of shit that I am." I gesticulated all the hand motions to match my words by faux ripping my heart out of my chest and throwing it to the floor and stamping on it.

"Holy hell, melodramatic much? Christ, Sydney. I'm telling you, it's all a misunderstanding. He's going to be waiting on your doorstep, flowers in tow, admitting this was entirely his fault. I promise."

"You can't promise. You don't know. You hate him, anyway. You want him to be gone."

"I don't even know him, hun. That is and has always been my greatest concern. I told you this was all happening way too fast.

Neither of you knew anything about each other. Here we are, not even a week later and he's gone. Was I wrong?"

"I told you. I made him leave. It's all my fault. Aiden has been nothing but wonderful and sincere and ..."

"And what? Mysterious? As far as I know, he still hasn't told you anything about himself, right? You wouldn't be panicking if he had. You have nothing on him, no way to reach him whatsoever. How do you know all this hasn't been his plan from the get go? Maybe he isn't who you think he is."

"I never would have made him leave if it weren't for you, you know. You've been planting things into my head about how he's hiding something from me since the first time I mentioned he moved in with me. You made me doubt him, and now he's gone." I pointed my finger at her face and squinted my eyes.

"You aren't seriously blaming me for this, are you? 'Cause I can tell you right now, that's not gonna fly with me. I have been by your side for how many years now? I've held your hair while you puked. You stood by me when I told my parents I was a lesbian and they accused you of being my lover. You stood next to Gina and I as our maid of honor the day we got married, when none of our family would stand by us. You'll be there the day we deliver our baby and through every day after. We've never had a fight, not even a misunderstanding, until this guy came into the picture. Now you're turning on me because I told you to look out for yourself and get to know him? Now he's gone and somehow it's my fault? I haven't even met him yet."

"And I guess you never will, since he's gone forever." I felt like the worst person in the world. Now I had hurt her, too. I didn't really blame her. I was responsible for my own thoughts and actions.

I held my head in my hands and the tears flowed freely. Hell, I was full-blown sobbing all over Cheryl's couch. She placed her arm around me and tried to comfort me with words of encouragement about meeting someone else, or things not being meant to be, or him coming back. I even think she recited the poem about loving something and setting it free.

"I'm sorry, Cheryl. I didn't mean any of that. It's not your fault. It's mine."

"Listen, babe, I know you're lashing out at me because you're hurting, and badly. And I forgive you for it. I remember doing the same thing to you at one point in time. Remember that day my family turned their backs on me? That's why we're friends. We have each other's backs. We're each other's sounding boards. So no, I won't hold any of this against you, but I might make you buy me lunch to make up for it. I love you. You're my best friend. You're my sister."

"I love you, too." I proceeded to soak her pajamas with my misery.

After my tears had subsided to sniffling and breath catching, Cheryl left to rifle through Gina's prescriptions to see if she could find me something to ease the pain. She returned with a hot cup of chamomile tea and a sleeping pill. Neither was going to stop the pain ripping through my heart right now.

"Take the pill and the tea. You need some sleep. I'm telling you, tomorrow morning everything will be back in perspective and you can reevaluate it all with a fresh mind. Trust me."

"*Trust me*. That's what Aiden asked me to do, and I didn't."

"Sydney, don't make me practice my mom skills on you. They're going to be mad skills and I don't think you want me to open them up on your ass right now. Take the damn pill."

She shoved her hand right in my face. It cradled a small white oblong pill. If Aiden didn't return to me, I'd consider taking the whole damn bottle. I slowly reached for the pill, hesitated, then realized I'd rather be sleeping than awake, living the torture I was presently experiencing. She dropped the pill into my hand and stood over me until she was sure I had taken it.

"Let me see under your tongue. I can't believe I have to do this. I'm going to get you a blanket and pillow. Sorry, babe, the couch is all I can offer you right now. We just don't have the room for guests. We're going to have to convert the office into a nursery as it is. I don't see us swinging a house right now or anytime in the near future. This whole pregnancy thing has cost us every bit of savings we had. I guess having a baby is more important right now than retirement. But isn't that always the case? Why keep it? You can't bring any of it with you once you're gone."

"I'm sorry. I'm ruining all your good news today with my problems and making you think about your problems."

"Oh honey, just you wait. Payback is a real bitch. I'll be on the phone with you at those three o'clock in the morning feedings. Believe me, you'll be getting phone calls at all sorts of ungodly hours."

As promised, Cheryl brought me a cozy blanket and pillow. She fluffed the pillow for me, patted it to suggest I place my head on it, and then tucked me in. She was going to be one fantastic mom. Hell, they both were.

"Okay, I'm going to head back to bed. I'm worried about you. Are you going to be all right?"

"Can you just stay with me? Until this stupid thing kicks in?"

"Hell yes! Want me to hold you?"

"Yes, hold me please."

Cheryl sat down on the couch end, and I rested my pillow and head in her lap. She stroked my hair until I dozed off. I'm not sure when she left, but it was before the nightmares started.

15

AIDEN

I must have been dreaming. It had to be a dream because I couldn't actually feel the pain I knew I should be experiencing.

I opened my eyes. Everything was so dark, and I was trying to adjust them so I could see. When my eyes were finally able to focus, I realized I was in my own bed at home. The sheets were soaked with sweat, and I was cold and uncomfortable. I sat up and ran my hand through my hair.

I remembered he was no longer in the room next to mine and began crying over his loss again. All of the pain rushed through me at once. My heart felt like it immediately stopped beating. It seemed each time I remembered he was gone; the shock of it hit me as freshly as it had when he walked out the door. I imagined it must be like that for a widow. Wake up from dreaming of your love, only to be hit with the hard reality they were gone and never coming back again. It must be torture. It was for me.

I pulled myself out of bed, feeling the uncontrollable urge to be in his room, as though it would let me feel him with me somehow. I threw myself down on his bed and began bawling. I tore at the sheets and wrapped them around me, so that I could pretend they were his arms that were holding me.

Although I was completely bundled up, I felt the temperature in the room plummet. I could see my breath as I sighed, knowing that had I not turned my back on him, he would be here with me now, keeping me warm and safe. Why was it so cold? I realized it was because my pajamas were soaked.

As I got up to change into a pair of sweats, I could feel someone was in his room with me, watching me. All the air pushed out of my lungs. My breath became stuttered as my heart stopped. I was frightened beyond belief. But my apprehension was soon replaced by what felt like relief.

That's when I began to feel like Aiden was there with me. I scanned the room to search for him.

He was standing in the darkest corner, only feet away from me. I could feel emotion pouring out of him and over me, almost as though he was trying to lessen my pain. It seemed to be working. His presence alone, knowing he was here with me, was enough to start my heart beating again. He had returned. After everything I had put him through, he came back to me.

"Aiden," I called out. He didn't respond. "Aiden, talk to me. I need to hear your voice. Please say something. Tell me you forgive me."

Again, there was no verbal response. I started to feel anger growing inside. More mind games? He just stared at me with a blank face. This whole thing was starting to verge on the edge of creepy.

"Stop whatever it is you're doing. Just come over here, and hold me, love me. Please. I need you."

His eyes softened and he smiled warmly at my plea, but made no move to come closer.

"Aiden, why are you doing this to me, to us?" I covered my face with my hands and cried. He was here with me, yet he wasn't. I wished he would stop messing with my emotions. I just wanted to feel his arms around me. I wanted to know he was real. I looked at him, but he was no longer there, and all the pain of his being gone spread back over me again.

I screamed for him. I couldn't move and wasn't sure if any sound was actually coming out of my mouth. Hands were on me and I nearly jumped out of my skin.

"Damn, you're the only person I know who can wake themselves out of a pill-induced sleep."

I groggily opened my eyes to find Cheryl hovering above me with a worried expression on her face. I was in her apartment, still on her couch. I must have been dreaming. I'm not sure if I could consider that a nightmare or not.

"When I mentioned being up at three-thirty in the morning, I was talking about the baby, not you. Close your eyes and go back to sleep before you're too awake. Then it'll be impossible to fall back to sleep unless I give you another dose. And honestly, that idea scares the shit out of me."

She tucked me in once again, shut the light off and left me alone. This would be my life now, alone without Aiden. Sleeping on my friend's couch. I knew I had done the wrong thing. I just had no way to take it back.

The rest of my night was uneventful. I believe I was able to sleep for a few hours with no nightmares. Occasionally, throughout the night, I felt like Aiden was there next to me, holding me. I would turn towards him, only to find he wasn't actually there, and the darkness would take hold of me again. I woke up before the sun, so I decided to take my leave and head home. I was dreading it, but I knew it was something I'd have to face at some point or another. I thought it best to get it out of the way now.

16

SYDNEY

When I drove up the driveway, I had a terrible foreboding feeling overwhelm me. I imagined again, this must be how a new widow feels coming home for the first time to a newly empty house. I'm not sure why I associated all of this with a widow instead of simply a break-up. It was probably because Aiden had been living with me. I knew I didn't have to worry about his things still being there. He'd taken what little he had with him. There was nothing left to hold or touch. I didn't even have any pictures of us together to reminisce over. *How could I not even have a picture of him? We had spent an entire day at the park and it never crossed my mind to take a picture?* Now I was kicking myself in the ass because it was too late. There would be no pictures of him or us together.

My house would simply be as it had been only days before, as if Aiden had never existed. Even from outside, my house looked empty. No, it looked more than just empty. It looked abandoned. There was no life to it at all.

I sat in my car in the garage, not wanting to move. I didn't feel like being alone. At least in the car, I could just rev it back up and leave with no effort. Once inside, I was afraid of being trapped there, with no one to help me or hear my cries. Silly really, to think I would feel that way. *I could leave whenever I wanted, couldn't I?*

I couldn't run away from being alone, though. I had been alone before Aiden and it had never bothered me like this. Even being at Cheryl's made me feel out of place, like a third wheel. It had never really occurred to me before, but with the baby coming, things were already changing.

After I while, I convinced myself everything would be fine. *How could one man in my life for only a few days change how I had lived for the past seven years?* I had been alone that entire time. I took my time gathering myself together, took a deep breath and withdrew from my car.

When I entered the house, it was so cold. The temperatures outside were quickly declining. Aiden had said we were in for an ice storm later in the week. For some reason that storm kept coming back into my mind. I would need to turn the heat on and shut the outside water valves so they didn't freeze. Aiden could have done that for me. Funny, we were only just at the park enjoying the warmth of the sun and each other and now everything seemed frozen. How easily thoughts of him being a part of my life had replaced my regular train of thought. The feeling overtook me and my hand shot up to cover my mouth. *Oh my God, Aiden was gone.*

The pain ruptured my heart almost as quickly as the fleeting vision of him had come to me. I felt like he had died. Having no way to speak, text or email him, it felt just like he had. No widow could reach out to a lost loved one, and here I was with no way to reach out to Aiden.

I had no idea where he was or who he was with. I had never given him Cheryl's friend's information. I thought about calling the base, but losing my job was not on the list of things I wanted to add to my misery right now. All they needed to do was get wind that Aiden was living here and I would be gone in mere moments. My performance record would be wiped clean. I deserved it. I had failed him. I had failed him in more ways than work.

I was only a shadow of myself now. There was no happiness and I felt there was no reason to exist like this. If I weren't so afraid of what awaited me in the afterlife, I would consider throwing myself off a bridge. I laughed at myself for even thinking about suicide. It wasn't the first time I had entertained the thought in the past twenty-four hours, but it was something I could never bring myself to do. I was a strong woman and certainly not a quitter. I knew it was my own way of feeling sorry for myself. I shouldn't, though; I should feel sorry for Aiden. What I had done to him was so cruel and heartless and I wouldn't blame him if he never tried to contact me again.

I wandered around my house like a lost soul, looking for anything that remained of him. There was nothing, not even a wrinkle in the comforter on his bed. It has been perfectly made so you could bounce a quarter off it. He had left nothing for me to hold, not a shirt or even a stray sock. I knew this would be the case, but actually experiencing it was quelling me.

I sat in the dreary light of the gray morning, my arms encircling myself, just so someone was holding me. I remained like this for hours, staring at nothing or crying hysterically. I continued to wait for him. He never came home. He never came back to me. I kept expecting the phone to ring or a knock on the door, but Aiden had completely vanished from my existence. *How was I going to live without him?*

Time was passing by so slowly. Sitting there in the silence of my house, I could hear every tick of every clock there was in the house. The clocks clicked at different times, causing a dissonant cacophony. I could count the seconds in my head. *One. Two. Tick. Tock.* I looked at the clock and only a mere hour had passed. When Aiden was with me, time always seemed to fly by. There weren't enough minutes available in the day when it came to being with him.

I started to pace around the room, straightening a book here or picture there. I wanted to touch anything he had touched. Even if his fingertips had just grazed something, I wanted it. I found myself sitting on the stairs, knowing we had climbed them together, only to wander back to my spot on the couch to pay more vigil for his return.

Every so often the heat would come on, but it never warmed me. Nothing made a difference. Everything just seemed so lifeless.

I hadn't eaten a single crumb since yesterday's lunch with the girls. The thought of food made my stomach lurch and only made me think about my last meal with Aiden. I had ruined that as well. *Why was I constantly sabotaging my own happiness?*

I sat and thought about that for a while. *Why did it matter to me what Aiden's past was? What difference would it have actually made? He wanted to be with me, right here, right now. I didn't know of any girlfriend or wife waiting for him, looking for him. Why couldn't I just be happy with what we had and who he was? No, instead I had to badger him for information; accuse him of hiding things. If anyone had the right to break up in this relationship, it was him. Which probably made it easier for him to walk out the door. He didn't beg me to stay, did he? But he had. He had asked me not to send him away. He had pleaded with me not to do it. I thought I was doing the right thing. I had forced him to go. What if he was only concerned about having a place to live? I don't even know if he had money for a motel. I was a disgrace. I was a heinous excuse of a human being.*

I could no longer sit and needed to do something. I turned on the TV, hoping to occupy myself with mindless nothing. I flipped through the channels, stopping on a news report focusing on a Marine killed that morning from my local region.

"Another one for Cheryl. Such a shame."

I listened as they gave the details of his bravery and demise. Happy pictures of him with his wife and child flashed on the screen.

"He had a family. They wanted him back and he'll never be able to come home. I had a man I could have spent the rest of my life with, and I sent him away. And here I am, acting like a selfish bitch, crying over my own stupidity, and feeling sorry for myself. That poor woman, she has the right to feel like she lost someone. I threw my someone away," I said aloud to the empty room. I winced at hearing my voice slightly echo.

I guess I should just suck it up, shake it off, and get back to the life I had *before* Aiden. It should be an easy adjustment. It's not like we'd been together for years, for God's sake. It had only been days. *What was wrong with me? Was I obsessed with him or something?*

I gathered my strength, plucked myself from the couch, and hauled myself to the kitchen. I turned on the tea water and scrutinized the contents of my fridge. Nothing jumped out at me. I decided to make toast with cashew butter because I needed comfort food.

I dropped the bread into the toaster and went for the flatware drawer. I removed a paring knife and began trying to cut the seal off the cashew butter lid. I must not have been paying attention because the knife slipped and plunged into my palm only inches from my wrist.

"Son of a bitch!" I screamed and pitched the knife into the sink.

The sharp pain that ensued brought a different kind of agony to my body. It made everything feel real. I saw the amount of blood streaming down my wrist and knew it was a deep cut. Good thing I had been a nurse before a poor excuse for a case manager. Blood didn't bother me in the slightest. I wrapped a clean dishtowel around my hand, collapsed onto the floor and began to turn on the waterworks again. It wasn't because it hurt, either. My hand *was* throbbing, but not enough to surpass the ache in my chest. I wished Aiden were here with me. Had he been, he would have been using the knife. He was, in his own words, a master in all forms of weaponry. I laughed through my tears, which only made me break down more.

The phone rang and I nearly jumped out of my skin. I waited to make sure it wasn't a figment of my imagination. It rang again. It sounded out of place, almost surreal. I jumped up and literally dove for it, praying it was Aiden. Hoping it wouldn't stop ringing before I could get to it. My aching hand was temporarily forgotten.

"Hello?"

No one replied. I could hear a strange noise in the background, but I couldn't quite place it. White noise? Did white noise even exist anymore with the age of digital we presently lived in?

"Aiden? Is that you?" I questioned, and then under my breath, "Please say something. Please be Aiden. Please. Please say something, anything." There was no response. I was reminded of my dream and Aiden's lack of response there, too.

The phone line went dead and the house returned to deafening silence. *Was my existence destined to be bleak?* I somberly placed the receiver back on the base, and decided I'd better attend to my hand. The towel was quickly becoming saturated with blood. I probably needed stitches. I'd decide once I cleaned the wound and could evaluate it better. I still had my nursing kit on the shelf in the closet, so maybe I'd just do it myself. It wasn't likely I'd be taking a trip to the hospital. Could this day get any worse? I bit my tongue after I said it. I probably just jinxed myself.

The upstairs bathroom had the best lighting, so I headed in that direction. Something was happening outside, but I couldn't tell if it was rain or wind. I peered out the front window. Rain. Yes, the day just got much drearier.

When I unwrapped my hand, the blood continued to flow freely from the gash. I ran lukewarm water over it and tried to gauge the depth. I had done a pretty good job on myself. Maybe I should have been doing covert missions on *my* tours. I was apparently deadly with a knife. Had I actually been trying, I could have done some major nerve damage.

I grabbed disinfectant and triple antibiotic cream, cleaned it up, and began working on steri-stripping it closed. Not an easy task to conquer using only one hand, which is why I had opted not to stitch it myself.

When I thought it was adequately done, I bandaged it back up and sat down on the bowl. From this vantage point I could see Aiden's empty room. It was completely dark except the pinpoint light shining from the bathroom, which caused an arrow effect right to his bed.

"Well, Aiden, if you had just made love to me, we'd probably still be in bed right now. But no, you had to go and tell me you loved me. I'd do anything to hear you say those words to me again right now." Again I found myself talking to no one, although I swear I had seen movement in his room from my peripheral vision.

Where was he? Who was he with? Was he thinking about me? I had no idea what the answer to any of those questions might be and they kept running through my head over and over again.

"Aiden, you said you loved me, yet you left me so easily. Where are you?" I screamed out to my non-existent roommate. My voice boomed through the empty house. It was now a cemetery and I was the widow, forgotten by everyone.

17

GINA

I was still sitting in the bathroom, probably for hours, when I heard a knock on my front door.

"Aiden, you came back." I flew down the stairs and flung open the door only to find Gina and a bottle of wine waiting for me.

"I won't be insulted that you don't look happy to see me. I'm guessing you thought I might be someone else?"

"Oh no, honey, I'm always happy to see you. How are you feeling, Momma? Come on in."

"Apparently a lot better than you," she said, gently taking a hold of my injured hand. "Trying to end it all but missed?" she said.

"Not really, but thanks for the idea."

"Oh stop it. See, that's exactly why I told Cheryl I needed to come over today."

"Don't you have classes?" I certainly didn't want her missing work on my behalf. I wasn't worth it.

"Don't you worry your dispirited little head about it. I have one of my other teachers covering for me. You're what's important right now. I can't have the Godmother of my child a wistful mess and sitting here desolate all day, now can I?" Gina tossed in my direction.

"Godmother?" I said excitedly.

"Of course, Sweetie. Who else would we want to be the Godmother? There's only one choice and it's you."

"Well, no one else seems to want me." It didn't take long for my depressed attitude to return.

"And again, stop it. Cher warned me you were all about the drama today. Here, I brought you this to take the edge off. We're going to sit and work this all out. Okay?" she exclaimed.

"But you can't drink," I scolded her.

"It's not for me, honey, it's for you, the whole bottle. From what I can tell after only a few minutes, I should have brought a whole damn case with me. Now inside, get a glass, and meet me on the couch!"

I did as she commanded and sat down on the couch with glass in hand. She already had the bottle open and waiting, and began to fill my glass to the rim.

"Okay. Take a deep breath, a large sip, and spill it. All of it," she demanded.

"Everything is a fucking mess. I really screwed things up. I doubted him. He told me he loved me and I didn't say anything back. I told him to leave. He reached for me and I turned my back on him. I made him cry. I suck! I'm the suckiest person I know. Now I don't have any way to reach him. I have no idea where he is or who he's with. I deserve to live alone in hell," I rambled.

"Good. Get it all out there. Feel any better?"

"Are you fucking serious?" I just glared at her. Her warm smile spread across her face and she giggled.

"No. I was only kidding. I know you don't feel better. We haven't solved anything yet. But at least you put it all out there on the table. I know exactly what I need to ask you to help." Her voice was soft and cheerful, as usual.

"There's no way to solve this. I have no way to find him," I told her.

"Let's start at the beginning. Yes, everything is a fucking mess. I have to say fucking because soon there'll be a governor on my cursing and I need to get it all out of my system. Fuck. Fuck. Fuckity. Fuck. Fuck. Now how is it that you feel you screwed things up?" I just kind of stared at her in disbelief. I had never heard Gina sound like a truck driver before.

"Did you hear a thing I said after that?" I asked.

"Drink. Yes, I did. You doubted him. Why?" I did as I was told and took a drink.

"Well, Cheryl kept telling me all these things and I started to think about them and realized she was right," I conceded.

"Well that was your *first* mistake. It's one thing to listen to someone else's advice, but it's ultimately up to you to make the decision of what to do with it. You didn't have to react to what she said. All you needed to do was take it into account, think about it and assess. Did you assess?"

"Yes. I ..."

"No, you didn't," she interrupted," You reacted. Don't lie to me." She waved her index finger in my face.

"Shit. I feel bad for your kid. You're one tough cookie and that child isn't going to get away with anything."

"No, I'm just blunt. I say what I think whether you like it or not. Don't ask my opinion if you don't want to hear it or the truth. I will always be nothing but honest with you. Now, did you assess?" she questioned again.

"No. I just got ... scared."

"Now we're making some progress. Drink. Do you really think deep down inside what Cheryl said was true? 'Cause you know, you can't lie to yourself. You always know it's a lie."

"No. I thought he was the most perfect man I had ever met and things between us were so easy." I took a gulp of my wine.

"So if you felt that, and you weren't lying to yourself about it, it must be true. Right?"

"But what if he ended up being what Cheryl said?" I questioned her this time.

"If no red flags jumped out, then I think you need to go with your own gut, not someone else's. She never even met him. She was being protective of you. You're not a big dater, so we're not used to you being with a guy. Plus you fell so fast. However, in life, you need to take risks, right? So if things felt right for you, then you just should have gone with your gut instinct. Drink. I suggest that's the way you go from now on. Heed other people's words, don't live by them."

"Thanks, Gina. That actually makes a lot of sense. I take it back. You're going to have the best advice for your kids. You're going to be one fuckawesome mom."

"Thanks, love. Now on to the next point. You said he told you he loved you and you didn't respond in kind. Is that about right?"

"Yes." I ran my finger over the rim of my crystal glass very quickly, trying to make it sing. Occasionally I would swirl it around and watch it form legs on the glass.

"Why didn't you say it back?" she challenged.

"I started to think about how I was supposed to be helping him and not seducing him."

"Nonsense. You can't help how you feel. Obviously he felt the same way or he wouldn't have said those words. So do you love him?"

"Yes. I love him. I love him *so much*. I even thought about having his child."

"Then what's the problem? If you feel it, you say it. Drink. So next time we see him, what are we going to tell him?"

"There won't be a next time." I finished the glass off and Gina immediately refilled it.

"Nonsense. You don't tell someone you love him or her, and

then never make an effort to win them back. He's either giving you space to think things over or he's letting you see how much you miss him. Guys are weird like that. So next time we see him, what are we going to tell him?"

"If I ever see him again, I'm going to tell him how much I love him."

"We're making *huge* strides. Drink. Now, you told him to leave. Why in hell would you do that?" Her voice was stern.

"I didn't want him to leave forever. I meant he should go stay somewhere else so we could see if what we had was real and not being forced. I thought being here with me all the time was just skewing his perspective."

"You don't have the right to tell someone how to think or what to feel. And you certainly can't decide what would be best for him without asking him. Am I wrong?"

"No."

"Okay, so we don't make decisions for other people because we think it's the best thing for us. We find out if it's the best thing for them, too. We didn't do that, did we?" The stern mother voice was still being slung in my direction.

"No."

"Then don't do that ever again. Drink."

"You do want me to be able to comprehend what you're telling me, right? I keep drinking like this and I'll be passed out on the floor at the rate you've got me going."

"Don't be ridiculous. It's wine, not tequila." She shook her head and rolled her eyes at me and then waited for me to sip the wine. I downed the whole glass and gave her a smug smile. She smiled sweetly back and refilled my glass to the top.

"Drink. On to the next point. He reached out for you and you turned your back on him. Really, Sydney? That's just terrible."

"Thanks, now I feel so much better."

"Again, 'honest thing' happening here. Why would you do that to any human being?"

"I don't know what I was thinking. I just figured if I stayed a minute longer, or reached back, he wouldn't have left. I was trying to make it easier on him."

"It sounds like you were trying to make it easier on you. We don't turn our backs on the people we care about. In fact, we don't turn our backs on anyone, ever. Do you understand me, young lady? I'm serious here. That's no way to treat another living thing." Again, with the finger wagging.

"I'm a terrible human being."

"Nope, just a selfish one. You turned your back to make things easier *for you*. Shame on you."

I held my hand out so she could slap my wrist. We both stared at the bandage.

"Nope, I don't need to. God already took care of it. What did you do, anyway?"

"I stabbed myself for thinking about eating."

"Brilliant. I should keep you around to help me lose weight after the baby. Now where were we?"

"I made him cry," I said flatly.

"Right. That's a tough one. Hearing a man cry is heartbreaking. I can silver-line it, though. Men only cry when it really hits them deep down. So he must really have some serious feelings for you if losing you made him cry. Wow, Sydney, I think that says a lot right there about whether he's genuine regarding his feelings for you. Don't you agree?"

Right there was a flicker of light for me. Gina *was* right, Aiden had cried over possibly losing me. That alluded to the fact that he truly meant what he said. He loved me. I was slightly dumbfounded for a moment.

"I'm good at this, aren't I? I mean, in your professional opinion."

"Better than I am, and I do it for a living."

"Stop putting yourself down. That reminds me, you do not suck, nor are you the suckiest person we know. You're just confused and scared. Those two things together bring us down some stupid roads."

"Stupid roads?"

"Sorry, I got carried away playing the part of a psychologist. Drink. I mean we make some really dumb decisions when we're confused or scared. Put them together and you have a recipe for disaster. Doesn't mean you can't fix it. And that brings us to our final point. How are you going to fix this, Syd?"

"I can't. I broke it." Gina laughed quite loudly at that comment. I side-eyed her.

"It's not broken. He loves you and you love him. Drink. It's just a matter of talking things out."

"There's the money statement right there, because that's a problem. There won't be any talking it out because I can't find him. I can't call him. And he hasn't come home."

Aiden coming home. The words were burning into my brain with searing pain. This was where Aiden belonged, with me in this house. This was *his* home. *Our* home. I broke down and sobbed into my hands.

"There, there, hun. Tears aren't going to do anything but give you puffy eyes. Can you call into the base and see if he checked in?

"No, they'll fire me."

"Look, there is another way, but you have to really have faith in it."

"Pray? I've been praying he'll come back since he left." I looked down at the floor when I said it.

"No, you have to reach him on a different level. Call him with your heart."

"What? Have you gone insane? Isn't it too early for baby brain?"

"I'm telling you, it works. Just go someplace that means something to both of you, like the first place you kissed or met. Then, just reach out to him with your heart and your mind. Make him *feel you*. Let him *feel* the pain you're in without him. Make him *feel the love* you have for him. Make him feel how much *you need him* to come back to you," she said confidently.

"I don't know, Gina. I love your whimsical side, but telepathically call him? Are you being serious?"

"Yes. Blunt over here, remember? Just try it. It can't hurt, can it?"

"No. I just ... I don't know if I can. I have no clue *how* to even start doing it."

"You'll do it once I'm not here. I know you will. Now I'm going to make you something to eat. Why don't you take a nice long hot shower, or maybe even a bath, and get yourself together. Because believe me, if he does come back, you don't want to look like you do right now."

"Thanks a lot."

She waved me off as she stood up, handed me the bottle and my glass, and then shooed me towards the stairs. I dragged myself up them and headed toward the shower. I looked in the mirror and realized she was one hundred percent correct. I looked like shit. My eyes had huge red rings around them, which made me look like a strung-out, hooker raccoon. My skin seemed translucent, like a thin veil or mask covered it. If Aiden came home to find me looking like this, he might turn right back around and run screaming.

I hated to admit it, but Gina was a huge help. I wasn't whining or wailing anymore. The depression still overtook me, but I had to believe that was normal.

I unwrapped my hand and stepped into the shower for a very long steamy time. The water seemed to help wash away the fatigue, at least. I opted for comfy clothing, putting on a pair of yoga pants and my Army sweatshirt. It made me feel closer to Aiden to be wearing it. Sometimes girls did silly things. I took a few minutes to blow out my hair and apply light makeup minus eyeliner. I even used waterproof mascara, knowing my tears weren't done yet. Even with makeup on, I still looked drained and miserable. I re-bandaged my hand and took something for the pain.

Gina was waiting for me in the kitchen with grilled cheese, bacon, and tomato sandwiches, kettle chips, and a pot of coffee.

"Well, that helped some. At least you don't resemble the walking dead anymore. I swear I thought you were going to eat my brains when I got here. Now sit and eat some food. It's time to get some sustenance into you. I made coffee against my better judgment, because I think you could use a nap right now."

Her sandwich was amazing. One of the best I'd had in a long time. I didn't often allow myself to indulge in things like melted cheese or bacon. I was always trying to eat healthy and watch my weight.

It took me a long time to eat. I just wasn't very hungry. Gina sat and ate with me, reminding me to take a bite every so often until the entire sandwich was gone.

"All right. We've worked things out. You're not crying anymore. You've been fed and cleaned up. I think my work here is done. I'm going to head home and leave you to figure out how to find Aiden. You can go traditional or my way. The choice is yours. I'll call later to check in on you. I'm going to come get you if you revert to your previous behavior. Do you understand me?"

"Yes, Ma'am." I felt tears start to well up in my eyes. *Ma'am. That's all it took.* I didn't want to take up any more of Gina's day, so I squelched the tears, put on a brave face and smiled.

"That's my girl. At least you're trying. You so know I can see right through it, though. It's okay. I still love you. See you later."

"I love you, too, and thank you, Gina. I don't know what I'd do without you and Cheryl."

"No reason to thank me. You've been there for us many times. Sometimes payback is a good thing. Look, even the weather is trying to cheer you up. I can see the sun starting to poke out from behind the clouds."

The sky did seem to be opening up, and rays of light were streaming down around my yard. I watched her walk to her car and drive away. I was almost afraid to close the door. It reminded me of closing the lid to a coffin. I would be alone again.

18

AIDEN

I wasn't quite sure how to approach it, but Gina was right, I was willing to try anything to reach out to Aiden. Since I had exhausted all traditional means of communication, I needed to try her suggestion.

So where could I go to feel centered enough to try and contact him? *My Zen.* Aiden had taken my backyard and made it into a place of Zen for me. The rain had stopped, so it was only a matter of grabbing my papasan cushion and a blanket. I settled myself into my chair, and pulled my knees up to my chest.

"Okay, here goes nothing. Aiden, please, come back to me," I expressed quite flatly and flopped my hands into my lap.

I felt like a complete idiot. This wasn't going to work. I might as well ask to win the billions from the lottery gods. I had about the same chance of either request working.

I needed to make this more real. I started to picture Aiden in my head, his warm smile, and the timbre of his voice, his beautiful eyes. *Wait, his eyes always seemed to reach into the depths of his soul when I looked into them. I'd focus on his eyes.* I imagined he was standing in front of me and I was staring right into them.

"Please, baby, come back to me. I am so, so sorry for asking you to leave. I didn't mean it."

I opened my eyes and nothing. I felt a pang of hurt, lowered my head and began to play with the hem of my pants. *Maybe if I just told him how I felt, really felt from the heart, he might hear me.*

"Aiden, I am so sorry for what happened between us. It's my entire fault. I was a complete and utter ass. I pushed you away right when I should have been pulling you closer. I wasn't honest with you." I said it with every emotion I had pent up inside me.

A breeze blew over me that chilled me right to the bone. I wanted to get up and hightail it inside but I wasn't done. I was actually feeling connected to him. Well, at least talking to him was making me feel like he was with me in spirit.

"Baby, I don't know how to find you. But I hope to God you can hear me, or at least feel me. I need you to know how I feel. I don't want you to be gone, because ... I can't live without you. Please, Aiden, come home to me."

"Sydney." It was almost as though I could hear his voice. "Sydney?" I heard it again.

"Please don't let me be hallucinating," I whispered under my breath.

"If you'd just turn around, you'd see that you're not." He chuckled from behind me.

I jumped out of my papasan, causing it to spin on its base, only to dump me flat on my stomach on the floor. The cushion and cage encased me, making me appear to be some sort of awkward, bizarre turtle. I was staring at a pair of shoes. Normally I might be humiliated at my display of gracelessness, but all I wanted to do was make sure Aiden's feet were in those shoes.

"Those are some awesome evasive maneuvers you have there. I would have been proud to have you as a member of my platoon."

I felt Aiden start to remove the cage from my back, but I quickly scrambled out from underneath it, and literally crawled up his body until I was back in a standing position and nestled into his arms.

"Aiden. You came back to me; you're home," I said through tears. I was grasping onto his shirt, holding him in place so he couldn't leave.

The waterworks were flowing so freely I was afraid I was going to drown him as I covered his face with kisses. I hugged him so close I was sure I was suffocating him, too. At this point, I was loving him to death, literally.

"Sydney, babe, I couldn't stay away from you even if I tried. Believe me, *I tried*. It took everything I had to stay away, so I could regard your wishes. I tried to give you what you wanted, but it's not what I want. I came here to beg you to reconsider. We can work this all out. I promise, I'll do whatever it takes to make you more comfortable."

"I don't care about any of that. I just want you here with me. You're a part of my life I can't live without. Please don't ever leave me again."

"I don't plan on it. Apparently you get violent when you're alone. What the hell did you do?" he voiced his concern while cradling my bandaged hand in his. He ran his fingers over my wrist and eyed me carefully.

"It's not what you think." I knew his initial impression was that I had tried to slit my wrist. It looked like I had, the way it was wrapped.

"I should hope not, Sydney. That would have been very detrimental to our future together," Aiden said sternly.

"I would never do that. I stabbed myself while trying to not starve myself."

"Very interesting way of going about things. I'm sorry."

"Why are *you* sorry?" I questioned.

"Because if I *had* been here, *that* wouldn't have happened. I hate the thought of you in pain in any way at all. I'm sorry I didn't come back sooner. Hell, Sydney, I'm sorry I left *at all*. I should have fought you to stay. I must have made you feel terrible, like I didn't care about you or want you. It's been torturing me since I walked out the door. I'm so sorry I hurt you like that."

"Again, why are you apologizing to me? I'm the one who hurt you. I *made* you leave. I told you to. I turned my back and listened while you cried over me. Please say you forgive me, Aiden. Please. I can't stand what I did to you. And I know I don't deserve your forgiveness, but if you could find it in your heart ..."

He placed his finger in front of my lips and shushed me. I felt like licking it. The feel of his skin touching mine was more than I could bear even from just his little finger alone.

"Have you eaten? Gotten any sleep at all? Does your hand hurt?" I was overwhelmed by his compassion for me after everything I had put him through.

"Gina came here and made me eat and shower. She took care of the cooking. Cheryl drugged me so I got at least three hours of sleep. Yes, it hurts, but I'll survive. How about you?" I smiled and waited for his reply.

"First things first." He took my hand, raised it to his mouth and placed a gentle kiss on it. All the pain seemed to melt away. "Yes, I've eaten. No, sleeping was not an option without you beside me. I've become spoiled in that respect. Does it feel better now?" he explained.

"Yes, actually it really does. Do you want to go inside? I can put on a pot of tea. Maybe we can talk things out or just hold each other for awhile." I didn't care where we were, really.

"I'd like to do all of it. I just want to be in your presence. Does that sound strange?"

"No. I completely feel the same way." And I did.

He took my good hand in his and led me inside. He brought me to the couch in the living room and sat me down.

"I'm making tea for you. I don't trust you in the kitchen right now," he teased. "You're hurt. I want to pamper you. Wait right here, I'll be right back. Don't move."

I nodded and watched him walk to the kitchen to begin making tea. I couldn't take my eyes off him. I was actually afraid to. I needed to be sure he was really here with me. I was also making sure he didn't ever leave again. The thought of barricading the door crossed my mind.

He returned while the water boiled, sitting right up against me and placing his arm around my shoulder. He pulled me close to him.

"Can I ask you a question?" I requested.

"You can ask me whatever you want. I won't hide anything from you ever again. I realized how it must have made you feel, my being so secretive."

"I shouldn't have pried," I told him.

"You had every right to, both personally and professionally. I was wrong to not be open with you."

"Where did you go? I mean, were you with anyone I ..."

"Stop right there. I would never run out and into the arms of another woman. So no, I was not with anyone. I went to a twenty-four hour diner. I spent a lot of time there. Sal, the owner and a very nice old *gentleman*, and I had a very long talk. You can thank him for helping me work some things out in my head. Very knowledgeable man."

My sigh of relief was probably louder than it needed to be. He smiled in response.

"I know the feeling. Gina missed her calling as a psychologist."

"I'm glad she was here for you. There's another reason why I didn't get any sleep. They don't take kindly to sleeping in diners," he joked. "Look, I'm sorry I didn't call you to let you know where I was. I just wanted to give you what you asked for. Space."

"I'm a fool. I had the best thing that ever happened to me right in front of me and I threw it away. I won't ever do that again. There is no *me* without *you*."

"You have no idea how true that statement is, Sydney. There is *no me without you,* either. Now I'm going to make that tea. Are you hungry?"

"No, thanks. I don't want anything but you. If the tea wasn't on the stove already, I'd say forget it, too."

The expression he had on his face was just so damn cute I couldn't resist pulling him into a kiss. His lips lingered on mine before he tore himself away to head into the kitchen. He returned shortly with a tray holding the pot of tea, two mugs and cookies. He poured us each a mug and handed mine to me.

"Ask me anything. What do you want to know?" I eyed him while trying to determine if he would sincerely answer anything I asked him.

"You don't have to do this," I told him.

"Yes, I do. Now ask."

"All right. Do you come from a big family?"

"I have two older brothers and my parents. Neither of my parents had siblings, so no cousins. So not really, just a very small family." That seemed painless.

"Do you miss them?"

"I miss them, but my parents weren't fond of my choice to join the military. It was really quite sad. They were opposed to war. They said if I partook in it, I was no longer their son in their eyes."

"Oh my God, that's terrible! How cruel. Whether people believe in war or not, every soldier deserves the respect and gratitude of their fellow man. Especially their family! You're the reason they have the freedom and lives that they do. If it weren't for our soldiers, we would live in a world of dictators and tyrants, unable to express who we are. Why can't people see that?"

"Yes, it's very sad that the very people we protect turn their backs on us."

"It's a crime. Treasonous, actually." I felt his pain. I was disgusted at the lack of respect for all soldiers by many.

"Maybe. The world we live in isn't what is used to be," he said.

"How about your brothers? Do you speak to them? Do you look like each other?" I was imagining two other beautiful men both resembling Aiden.

"No, we all look quite different. My brothers each went their own way. As time passed, we lost every day contact and soon it became a call for a birthday or a card for Christmas," he explained, disheartened.

"I didn't have any siblings. I guess you don't miss what you've never known or had."

"We were never really that close. They were quite a few years older than me. They were already in college when I was only in grammar school. Were you close with your parents?"

"Yes, very. I loved my parents. We were very close. I shared everything with them. This is their house. You already know they're both dead now. They died in an auto accident when I was only twenty-one."

"Syd, I'm so sorry."

"It's cool. It was a long time ago. And anyway, I feel them here in the house sometimes. Their presence, you know? I haven't felt it for ... well, for quite some time now."

"Maybe they moved on because they saw you were going to be all right and knew you eventually wouldn't be alone."

"I like the idea of that. Yes, that's the way I'm going to think about it from now on. I wish they could have met you. I bet they would have loved you. My father was in the military, too. I had their total support in everything I did."

"You're very lucky to have had such loving and supportive parents."

"Yes, I really was. More, please. Where did you grow up?" I was thoroughly enjoying our sharing.

"I grew up in a very small town on the west coast. I don't even think it would show up on a map it was so small. I did grow up by the beach, though. Spent a lot of my youth there surfing."

"You surf? That's so awesome. I'm jealous. I wish I were coordinated enough to surf. Plus I'm pretty sure I'd be a shark magnet."

"Well, this shark sure wants to take a bite out of you," he said in a sultry smooth voice.

And that one small statement changed the entire dynamic for the rest of the night.

"Oh? You want to eat me?"

He growled, took my tea and dropped it onto the tray. His hands were on me in a second and I was soon underneath him.

"You have no idea how tasty you look."

"I'm sure those cookies weren't as filling as I could be. What's stopping you?"

"Nothing!" I was expecting a feverous kiss, but what I got instead was the most tender and sweet pressing of his lips to mine. He held himself up on one elbow while petting my cheek and caressing my hair. Our eyes were locked, and the familiar hum was more intense than ever before.

"Sydney," he whispered my name reverently.

"I love you, Aiden."

"Sydney, you don't have to—"

"Yes I do, because I do. I love you, Aiden. I don't ever want to live without you. Please say you feel the same way."

"You know the answer to that already, don't you? How deeply I feel for you with everything I am. Without you, I'm nothing, so I have no plans of ever leaving you again. I told you once before, I can't exist without you, but it has to be because you want to be with me. Because you *choose* to be with me forever."

It made my heart hurt slightly that he didn't say the words back to me. Who could blame him? The last time he did, I pushed him away. It was my turn to tell him how I felt.

"I do choose you. I only lost you for one night and I could barely survive. You're like air to me. I can't live without it or you," I told him.

He reached over, pulled me close to him, and placed a sweet kiss on the top of my head. We stayed wrapped around each other, no words needing to be said. Each other's presence alone was all we needed.

19

CHERYL

Around seven, the phone rang. I already knew it was Cheryl and Gina checking in on me.

"Are you going to get that?" he asked.

"It's the girls making sure I'm still alive."

"Then you should answer it. They deserve to know you're fine. They were there for you. I want them to know how grateful I am to them for that. Please, tell them."

"Okay." I answered the phone and both were on the other line.

"How are you, Sydney? We're both very worried about you. Do you want us to come over or do you want to come stay with us tonight?" Cheryl asked.

"I love you both so much. But no, right now I have company."

"Oh? Do tell?" Cheryl said.

"I took Gina's advice and called him to me. And it worked. We should change your name to Gina-eous. He's here with me now. We've been talking things out. Everything is good, *so good* right now."

"Yay! I'm so excited. See? Everyone makes fun of me, but when you have a connection with someone that's too strong for the boundaries of this world we live in, you can touch them with your soul. Cheryl knows. She might not admit it, though. Sometimes I send messages to her with my heart and it never fails, she always calls me within ten minutes."

"Stop doing that, Gina. I'd call you anyway." Cheryl was laughing as she said it.

"Well, sometimes I'm in a class and I need you to stop and get milk, so I tell you with my head. You always come home with milk," Gina revealed to Cheryl.

"Now you're just freaking me out. If I get thoughts about buying you expensive things, I'm going to ignore it."

"Ladies, listen. I have a message for you both from Aiden. He wanted me to tell you how grateful he is that you were here to take care of me. He was very touched by your love and concern."

"Tell them that I never would hurt you intentionally like that. I was only following your wishes," he whispered to me.

"He also wants you to know he would never hurt me like that. That he was only doing what I asked. And that he will never hurt me again."

"Well, let him know we appreciate that and we would never let our girl hurt through something like that alone. And we understand his side and we forgive him."

I opened my mouth to repeat their words, but Aiden waved me off. We were sitting close enough he could hear them. They were both loud talkers."

"Okay, we're going to let you two have some more time to talk. Call us if you need anything, babe."

"I love you both so much. Thank you."

"We love you too, honey. You don't have to thank us. We're always here for each other. That's just how the three of us roll. You let Aiden know that we're really looking forward to meeting him."

"I will. Love you. Bye." I hung up and focused my attention

back to Aiden. This was the right time. There would be no more waiting. I needed him in every way. I needed him completely. Down to my very soul.

20

AIDEN

"Would you like to open a bottle of wine and talk some more? I'm not really into tea at the moment."

He smirked and immediately went to my wine rack. Not actually the rack I wanted him to go for, but the wine was all part of my plan to make this the right time. I wanted him and I needed his inhibitions down.

He returned with a bottle of vanilla vodka, two glasses, and some guava juice I had in the fridge. *Even better.* We drank as we shared stories about our childhoods. But eventually I was reminded of work and decided to shift the direction of our conversation.

"Why did you join the military?"

"Because I wanted to honor all the men and women before me who gave their lives for my freedom. I wanted to give back and also to carry on what every soldier in the history of this country gave to me. Freedom."

"That's beautiful, Aiden. I know you've made every single one of them proud."

"Why did you join the military?"

"Because of my father, grandfather, and uncles. They were all in the military. I'm the last one, you know. After me, there's no one else to carry on our name. Anyway, I wanted to give something to those soldiers who were wounded. I didn't want them to feel like they were alone. Whether they survived or not, I wanted to be the one who held their hands when they might be afraid. I guess I could keep that secret for them. Sometimes they told me other things, too. Secrets aside from their fear of dying or messages for their loved ones, if they had one. And I made sure that every single message they gave me made it home even if they didn't."

"I want to give you something. Can you wait right here?" he said, getting up.

"Of course."

Aiden ran up the stairs and moments later, was bounding back to my side. In his hand he held a small black box with a military insignia on the front of it. He held the box out to me. I stared at it for a moment; a strange pit in my stomach, like every girl must feel when she thinks the box contains a ring. I knew from the shape it didn't, but I hesitated just the same. He could have been made of stone, because he didn't move a muscle until I reached for the box.

I held it in my hands and admired it before lifting the lid. I finally mustered the courage to see what was inside. It held his Purple Heart. I had to force myself to look away from it and into his eyes. I wasn't sure of the gesture he was trying to make. My face must have clued him in to my cluelessness.

"I want you to have it."

"No, Aiden. You earned this. I can't take this from you."

"But don't you understand? My heart only beats today because of you. It's my heart and I'm giving it to you. Also, for being there for every soldier you helped *move on to a different kind of life*. Because you know I believe there is more after this one. You helped them make that transition with your kindness. You deserve this medal as much as I do."

The significance of this gift was immeasurable. I held it against my own heart and kissed him. At that point, everything was forgotten except for kissing that man. I couldn't hold myself back anymore. I needed him to know how much that gesture meant to me. How much he meant to me. I was quickly on my back and he was on top of me.

His hands moved all over me. Soon, he was slowly removing my shirt. He did it so reverently. He kissed and caressed every inch of skin that he exposed like it was a piece of gold from a lost treasure.

Our movements became feverish and soon we were heading up the stairs, leaving a trail of my clothing in our wake. There was no way we were going to get as far as his room, so we ended up in mine. He swept me off my feet and gently placed me on the bed. He was soon next to me and we continued to ravage each other.

"Aiden. Make love to me. I want ... I need to make love to you. Please don't say this is the wrong time. I can't—"

"Shhh. You don't have to beg me. I can't resist you any longer. You're the only reason I breathe; the only reason my heart beats."

An extremely sexy smirk covered his face as I felt his hand run down to my panties. His finger ran along the waistband, teasing me, and he began to slowly tug them down. When he reached my sex, his fingers grazed over my lips and he slid his fingers up and down them. I was so wet that even his fingers alone felt like heaven. I wanted him inside me so badly. A small moan escaped me, which made him groan along. The sound of his desire for me brought me into a frenzy, and a new level of hotness to our foreplay ensued.

He quickly pulled my panties off and threw them to the side of the bed. I was completely unclothed now. He was still fully dressed. I felt like I belonged completely to him, his personal concubine, here for his every whim and desire. It made me hotter than I already was. I spread my legs slightly apart, to let him know anything was a possibility and I wanted it all.

His mouth began exploring my body. He started at my neck and slowly worked his way down to my breasts. He held onto them as his lips gently caressed them, suckling them. My skin prickled under his touch. Continuing, he ran his tongue down to my stomach, moving ever so slowly, licking every inch of my skin. When he finally reached his destination, I was dying for him to take a bite.

He had one hand on my breast and another between my legs. Soon his mouth was on my sex. He made lazy circles over it with his tongue, stopping only to suck on it gently, while he worked me with his other hand. Every part of my body he wasn't concentrating on ached for his attention. My exposed skin screamed to be touched, kissed, and tasted. I could hold back no longer.

I begged him, "Aiden, I want to feel you, all of you, against me, your skin against mine. I want you inside me. Take off all of your clothes, every last stitch. Please, you have to make love to me right now."

He smiled at my pleading tone, and complied quickly. I helped unbutton his pants while he pulled his shirt over his head. His body was amazingly muscular. My wondering mind had done justice to it. He was everything I had imagined him to be. This man was one sexy piece of ass and he was in my bed about to make love to me. My heart exploded in my chest.

He lay down next to me and played with a strand of my hair. I believe he was trying to calm himself before we moved any further. I was having a hard time controlling myself. Next to me lay the man of my dreams, both of us naked. I had to feel skin to skin. I looked at him from under my lashes, my lids heavy with desire for him, and silently mouthed the word *please.*

He pulled me on top of him. I need to touch every inch of him. I began to run my fingers lightly down his chest and something stopped me. I felt a deep divot. My fingers hovered over it. It had to be one of the scars from the four bullets he had taken in the chest. His body immediately tensed.

"Is this one of the places you were shot?" His eyes left mine as he looked down.

"Yes. I'm so sorry. It's not ..."

"It's not what? Sexy? It's beautiful, Aiden. It's a medal of honor. You took that bullet and saved so many others' lives. You gave all those men a chance to be with their families. You have that scar for everyone's freedom. It's extremely sexy." I leaned down and placed a soft kiss on it.

I ran my hand over his chest again; probing for his remaining *medals*, and found two others. I kissed each one in turn. I continued with my search over his skin and finally found the last scar. It was right over his heart. I stopped; my fingers shook as they hovered over it. I looked into his eyes. There were tears there. There were in mine as well.

"Sydney." His voice was soft and breathy. It gave me chills to hear him, to feel that scar, so deep. Goosebumps broke out all over my body.

"Aiden. You took a hit directly to your heart? How the hell are you still alive?"

"Right now, it's you that makes me feel alive, like I never have before. Sydney, I ... I think ..." he hesitated.

"Aiden. Say it. Say it out loud. I want to hear it, I'm ready to hear it now."

"I'm falling in love with you, Sydney. What I mean is, I'm already there." He looked shyly at me, like I would push him away again. But my heart exploded in my chest again and tears formed in my eyes.

"Aiden. Do you honestly love me, not just the idea of me?"

"Yes, Sydney. I think I fell in love with you the second I saw you. I've said that before. I hope you believe me now."

"Aiden, I feel the same. I'm in love with you. I've never felt this strongly about anyone in my entire life. I don't think I ever will again. You're my click."

"Your click?"

"The one. You're the person I'm supposed to be with. There's no other explanation. You're my soul mate. I love you, Aiden."

"It's you and only you for me, it's always been you. I feel so lucky to have this chance to be together."

"I'm the lucky one. This really does have to be fate."

"It's our destiny."

He rolled me onto my back and he crushed his lips to mine. I crushed right back. I slid my tongue into his mouth and pressed my body as hard as I could into his. I wanted to pull our bodies into each other and make them one. I couldn't get him close enough to satisfy my thirst for him.

Our kisses became frantic and our hands began to touch anything we could reach. He reached down to my breasts and began to massage them with his hands. He kissed my nipples and sucked on them. His tongue made small circles and he would then bite them gently. I arched into him to give him more access. I moaned in pure ecstasy.

"Make love to me now," I whispered into his ear before I began to nibble on it. He groaned and I felt him nestle himself between my legs. He was right at my entrance and he was hot and very hard. I began to ache even more for him. He slid himself up and down my folds. I ground my hips into him, needing to feel more friction.

He removed himself from my body and pulled me to my feet. He pushed me up against the wall, picked me up, his hand supporting my bottom, and I instinctively wrapped my legs around his waist. I had to have him now.

"Please, Aiden, I want to feel you inside me. I need to feel you inside me." He plunged hard and deep at my request. My entire body began to tingle. It felt like he was making love to every single cell in my body.

His mouth covered mine in a passionate kiss, and he held my face in place. His entire body and soul seemed to encompass mine. There wasn't anything I wouldn't give for this man. I wanted to give him everything, every part of me. He owned me.

He was strong, yet gentle and was completely focused on what was happening between us on every level.

"Oh God, Sydney, you feel so amazing. I can't ... Oh, I—" He was lost in our lovemaking as well, unable to say what he was feeling. I was in the same boat. This was like nothing I had ever experienced before.

He thrust slowly in and out of me, kissing me with each move. I was grinding back into him, trying to move faster. The feel of him was so intense I couldn't help myself.

"Slow down, Sydney. I want this to last all night if at all possible. If you keep moving like that, it's only going to be seconds."

"I can't help it. You feel so good. Oh, Aiden. I just can't stop myself. I can't get enough of you."

We fit together like puzzle pieces. Whether we were making love, holding hands, or just holding each other, it was as if our bodies were made for each other. He fit me perfectly in every way. Each time he pumped into me, he hit the right spot, and my body would shudder with what I could only explain as the beginning of an orgasm. But then, it would slow right before I went over the edge. I grabbed his ass; *oh it was so muscular and perfect*. I felt it flex each time he pushed into me. He was intoxicating. I felt high. I could only respond by pulling him deeper into me.

He moved us onto the bed so he could get better access. Once there, his groans became increasingly louder. I ran my tongue down his neck, wrapped my fingers into his hair and pulled him to me. I began to bite his neck gently, sucking and licking. I wanted more of him. I couldn't figure out how I could *get* more of him. My lips searched for his and I sucked his lower lip into my mouth. I tugged at it with my teeth and swirled my tongue over every inch of his. I felt out of control. I just wanted more, more, and even more. I felt the familiar tightening deep down and soon I was having wave after wave of the most intense orgasm I had ever had. Aiden watched my face the entire time.

"Sydney, I'm going to come. I can't hold back anymore. Just watching you like that. You're so sexy. Knowing that it's me who's pleasuring you."

"Aiden. I want to feel you come."

The thought of him coming inside of me drove me insane and I began to slam myself against him harder and faster. He grabbed onto the top of my headboard and began to drive into me. Within moments he let out a loud moan, buried himself as deep within me as he could possibly get, and began to shudder with me.

We lay there together panting, kissing, and still touching each other everywhere. I was ready to go another round.

"Aiden. I don't know how to express how I'm feeling right now. That was just—"

"I know. I can't explain it, either. Maybe we should do it over and over again until we can find the right words."

I smiled while tousling his hair with my fingers. We stayed in bed together just kissing and holding each other for a while longer until my stomach began to growl.

"Hunger. Food."

"That sounds like a fantastic idea, but just something quick. I plan on *this* being the rest of our week's activity."

We got dressed, *sort of*, if you count wrapping sheets around us as being dressed, and pranced downstairs to grab sustenance in the form of leftovers, snacks, and drinks. We brought it back upstairs.

That was pretty much how we spent the entire night. Making love, talking, noshing on snacks, and then making love again. We spent a lot of time just staring at each other. No words exchanged between us. I never met a man who could turn me on using eye contact alone, but Aiden had it covered. It was the cause of at least three love making sessions. I couldn't keep my hands off him.

At some point, being extremely content and exhausted from making love into the wee hours of the morning, we drifted off to sleep. He kept his arms wrapped around me, as if he was afraid that if he let go, I would vanish. I had no intentions of going anywhere. All I wanted was to be right here, in his arms, forever.

―――

When the day's light began to creep into the room, we began

making love all over again. We stopped at some point to take a nice hot bath. I was almost sore from the sexual calisthenics we'd performed most of the night. I thought it would be a good time to do a quick call in.

"I'll be right back. I have to check in with work."

"Well, I'm certainly not going anywhere. I'll be right here waiting for you. I'll get the bath all set up," he said sweetly.

I gave him a huge grin and ran to grab my cell to call Cheryl and Gina. *Work shmirk*. After showing up at their door as a sad excuse for a living creature, and making them listen to me cry incessantly, they deserved to know what had been happening at my house since Aiden's return. I wanted to share my high spirits with them. I needed to squeal in delight with my girls.

21

CHERYL

"Well, hello there, Sydney. So how's life with your soldier boy going?"

"Cheryl..."

"You had sex with him. I can hear it in your voice."

"How did you ... never mind. All night and all morning. I only took a break to call you. I had to squeal like a little girl with someone."

"Okay, I'll squeal this one time, but Gina is the one you should call. She'll want every single detail. Squeal," she said without any enthusiasm at all.

"Nice, Cher. It was so amazing. Like nothing I've ever felt before."

"You don't get around much, do you?" Cheryl's sarcasm never left her side.

"No, I don't. But from what I do remember about sex, it was nothing like this at all. This was just ... indescribable."

"Well, don't get all dick-whipped on me now. I still want you to take things slow, not jump into bed with him the second he came back to you. Although, let me give you some claps of approvals there, too. Didn't think you had it in you. You slut." She laughed this crazy laugh to make it sound evil. I giggled back.

"Okay, well, I better get back upstairs before all the bubbles disappear."

"Bubbles?"

"We're taking a bubble bath."

"Oh man, you're so gone. I can't wait to meet this guy."

"Well, tonight's finally the night. Promise me you'll behave!"

"I'll do no such thing. That would be out of character for me." She was quite serious, even though there was an edge of sarcasm to her statement.

"Really? Do I need to call Gina about that, too?"

"No, I'll behave, to a degree. I won't interrogate your soldier, if that's what you mean. I might make idle chitchat with him and ask him where he's from. Is that going to be an issue?"

"As long as there are no bright lights or water torture, I'm fine with it. We've talked about a lot of things. He's not holding back anymore," I told her.

"Look, I know this guy means everything to you. I'm pretty sure you're living my past. This is just like I was with Gina. Don't think I didn't see how miserable you were when he left. I've never seen you like that in all the years I've know you, and to tell you the truth, I don't ever want to again. Being without Aiden doesn't become you," she admitted.

"And this means?"

"This means I'm going to restrain the best I can and try not to butt in. I can't make any promises, though."

"I'll take it. And Cheryl?"

"Yes, my dear?"

"I wanted to thank you and G again for being there for me, this time in private. I know this whole thing is so not like me at all. Even when you were completely against Aiden and I jumping into things, you still helped me at my lowest point without telling me you told me so."

"Are you getting all sentimental with me? I'm so not going there," she said, half kidding. Cheryl was not all about the warm fuzzies.

"Cher, please. I want you to hear this. You're my family, both you and Gina. I mean it. You're like my sister."

"So that makes Gina your sister-in-law?" she chuckled.

"No, she's my sister, too. I feel like the bond we have is what I knew having siblings would be like. I want you to know my will states that if anything happens to me, you and Gina get this house."

"Stop it. You're freaking me out. Don't talk like that."

"But I want you to know. It's a done deal. And I also want you to list me as the guardian for the baby, if something should happen to you both. I promise you I'll raise your child like you would have," I said, the words coming from deep within my heart.

"Please don't. I feel sorry for this kid already having me as one of its parents."

"Shut up. Don't put yourself down. You showed me exactly the kind of parent you're going to be. Both of you did. That is the luckiest child in the world, getting the two of you."

"Stop, you're actually making me blush. And as you very well know, that's not an easy thing to do."

"I most certainly will not stop. You need to hear this. This little baby will be surrounded by so much unconditional love. She will know what love really is. Not just by watching you and Gina together, but seeing how you come to her side, no matter what. Even if it's something you don't agree with, you'll be there to hold her and make it all better. She's so lucky."

"So your call is it's going to be girl?" Out of everything I said; she focused on the one thing that wasn't a compliment to her. So typical of Cheryl.

"Oh I don't know. It's just what came out. It's what I felt. She. I feel a little girl is on her way to us. Yeah, that's my call. I just know it's a little girl. It's almost like there's an angel whispering it into my ear."

"An angel, huh. That's because you've been in heaven for the past few hours."

"Yeah, I have. What time are you coming over?" I asked.

"I think somewhere around seven. Is that too late, too early?"

"Nope, it's perfect. Gives me a few more hours to have sex!"

"Goodbye, Sydney. I can hear your bubbles popping."

"Goodbye, Cheryl."

22

AIDEN

It was the perfect day to stay home and in bed, especially with Aiden. The weather was terrible. I could hear the small pellets of sleet hitting the roof and windows. I moved the curtains back to take a peek outside. It was gray and somber.

"Don't look out there. It's much warmer inside here with me," Aiden whispered into my ear as he came up behind and wrapped his arms around me.

"Warm would not be my choice of wording. I'd say it's pretty hot in here and about to get a lot hotter."

"Yes, it is. Our bath awaits you, Madame."

"I'm very excited about it, too. You can reach all the hard to scrub spots."

"I plan on making sure every inch of you is squeaky clean."

After we took our bath, we put on comfy clothes and then took them off again for sex, and then put them back on. This was the way it seemed to go. I ordered lunch in from the local deli, the only one that actually delivered.

I was so happy to be cuddled up with Aiden the entire day. Presently, we sat in bed playing dirty scrabble.

"That *is not* a word," I said.

"It most certainly *is*," he countered.

"What the hell does it mean?"

He reached between my legs and pointed.

"You're kidding me? I never heard it called *that* before."

"You don't get around much, do you?" he laughed.

"Now that I *have* heard."

"I'm really glad you don't have to go in to work. The weather looks really bad. The roads are probably treacherous."

"I agree. It's really looking icy out there." We were snuggled on the couch, feeding each other gooey homemade oatmeal chocolate chip cookies over our board game, when I received a phone call from work telling me I needed to pick up important paperwork for Aiden's case. I had completely forgotten about him being a case at all. In my head, he was my lover, my boyfriend. *Hell, he was my future husband.*

"I guess you spoke too soon. I have to run in to work. They have some of your final paperwork that needs to be signed so you can become civilian again. And officially mine and not the Army's anymore."

"Sydney." He looked distraught.

"What's wrong? I'll be right back. Are you missing me already?"

His face took on a tortured look and I was starting to worry about his reaction to my leaving.

"Sydney, I would be so happy to stay like this forever with you. But..."

"I'm already not liking the 'but' part." I was now afraid that if I left, he'd be gone when I got back. I didn't want to go through that again.

"Sydney, you have a life here and I can be part of it to a certain capacity, but not completely. I want to start over. Start over completely from scratch with you. Come away with me."

"Aiden, I don't understand what you're saying. Why can't you be a part of my life here? I hate the thought of leaving Cheryl and Gina, and of course, the baby is on the way, too. I want to experience the whole pregnancy and birth with them. I mean, you're already here and you have nothing holding you to anywhere else, right? Is there something I'm not aware of? Should I be concerned about the paperwork I'm picking up? Is there a hidden wife somewhere?"

The second I started to doubt him again, he flinched, like my words had burned him. He seriously looked in pain.

"Aiden?" I rubbed my hand up and down his arm to console him.

"Sydney, there's no one but you. I promise you that. I just don't think this is the best place for us. We can go anywhere we want to. Do anything we want. Just not here."

"I'm not opposed to it. I think we can talk about it more. I can't imagine letting you walk away from me again, so yes, it's a possibility." This seemed to relieve him and he smiled and caressed my cheek.

"My beautiful Sydney, I know you have to go. I hate to let you leave, though."

"I'll be back before you know it. Gina and Cheryl are coming over to meet you tonight, so I really won't be long because there's no way I'm leaving you alone with those two. They'll tear you to shreds!" I laughed so he'd know I was really only kidding, although they would have a blast with him.

I threw on more appropriate clothing and when I got to the bottom of the stairs he was waiting for me. He pulled me tight and crushed his lips to mine.

"Wow, that's some hell of a goodbye kiss. I'll only be gone an hour. Really. Unless ... are you going to be here when I get back?"

Now I really was worried he would leave again. I didn't want him to. I was starting to feel panicked.

"I'm never going to leave you. Not even if you asked me to. I can't. It's not possible. I'm bound to you."

"I feel the same way. I want to be with you forever." I ran my hand down his cheek and softly kissed his lips in the sweetest way I possibly could to say goodbye for now. I wanted him to know I was coming back to him and soon.

23
CHERYL

The roads were complete crap. I was driving as slowly as I could because there was black ice everywhere and my car was sliding at every turn I made. I hated driving in icy weather, especially in such a small car. My fifteen-minute drive turned into half an hour. There was no way I was making it home in an hour as I had promised Aiden. He had looked so worried when I left the house. I thought about calling him to let him know I had arrived safely but it slipped my mind once I finally pulled into my parking space. I drew in a deep breath of relief. I hadn't realized how scared I had been the entire trip here.

When I finally reached my office, I ran to my desk, but there was no paperwork anywhere to be seen. I checked my inbox ... nothing. I ran to the mailroom to check there. Nothing. *What the hell?*

I took this opportunity to head over to see Cheryl.

"Hey there, babe."

"What the hell are you doing here? I'm surprised you can even walk the way you said you were going at it."

"Ha. Ha. That's very funny. You're a laugh riot. Did you ever think of becoming a professional comedian? I received a call at home telling me that I needed to come in and pick up some paperwork for Aiden to sign. But I can't seem to locate it."

"Isn't it there?"

"Nope, it's MIA. So are you excited to meet him?"

"Oh yeah, I want to meet the man who has my girl tied all up in goofy love knots."

"Well, you only have to wait a couple of hours now. I'm preparing him. So be nice!"

"I promise to be nice. I'm always nice." I shot her a *who-the-hell-are-you-kidding* look. "Whatever," she said flatly.

"Listen, I want to tell you something now, so you don't freak out tonight if it comes up."

"What now? Let me guess, you're pregnant?"

"Right, I got pregnant sometime between this morning and last night, and I already know." I rolled my eyes at her.

"Fine. Tell me."

"Aiden and I are in love. I mean full-blown love. Words said and everything."

"Well, I figured that was coming so I'm not surprised. Is that the big news?"

"No, but it's a part of it. He asked me to move away with him so we can make fresh start for both of us. Together."

Cheryl's face went blank. I found this completely disturbing. It meant she was about to blow a gasket.

"What? Are you fucking kidding me? Why? Why in the hell would you do that? Why would you even consider it? Why would he even suggest that? Is he hiding something?"

And there it was, the blown gasket.

"I don't think so. I think he just wants a fresh start. Together. No one's past to get in the way. I'm even thinking it might be a good time for me to leave the military, too. I've been toying with the idea of opening a private practice. I think I've been spoiled lately, not having to come into the office."

"I don't like this one bit. You meet this guy and in less than a week you're in love, then he's gone, then he's back and now you're moving away together? This doesn't sound bizarre to you?"

"It did. But then I thought about it and I don't want to be without him. We've already seen what affect that had on me. I told him it was worth further discussion. I mean, I'm not tied to this place. I could rent out the house. Hell, you and Gina have been looking for a place. You can take my house over. It's already going to you, anyway."

"I can't believe *I'm* even having this discussion with you. This is ridiculous. When did this all happen? Last night? This morning?" she quizzed me.

"Why does it matter? Look, Cher, I have no family left. I only have you and Gina here. I could have the chance to move someplace beautiful and warm all year round. You know how much I detest the snow and ice."

Cheryl just glared at me, shaking her head, while she tapped her finger on the table. She was most likely trying to think of what to say next.

"Please, Cheryl. Just keep an open mind about all this. I'm not saying I'm leaving tomorrow."

"He just comes out of nowhere, with no past to speak of, moves into your life and your house, breaks your heart, and then shows up, only to want to kidnap you. Who the hell is this guy?"

"Aiden," I said flatly.

"Aiden what? You never even told me his last name." Cheryl was furious. She was no longer butting out of this situation.

"Are you planning on running a background check on him or something?" I accused her.

"Maybe. I do have the clearance, you know."

"Cheryl, it's really not—" I wasn't allowed to finish my sentence. I felt like a child being scolded by a parent.

"Tell me his *full, real* name. I want to know exactly how it was listed on his paperwork," she demanded.

"Sergeant First Class Aiden Thane."

I watched as all the color drained from Cheryl's face. She looked like she was going to throw up.

"Are you okay? What's wrong with you? You look really pale right now." I was starting to seriously worry about why she was having that reaction. My stomach moved into my throat.

"Sydney, did you just say Aiden Thane? Sergeant First Class *Aiden Thane?*"

"Yes. Why?"

"I have his file," Cheryl looked visibly upset.

"What? That's ridiculous. Why would you have his file? You only deal with the deceased. It has to be a mistake. He's obviously not dead. He's at my house. I just left him there."

She picked up a file from behind her. She started to read from it. Her hands were shaking.

"Sergeant First Class Aiden Thane. Purple Heart. The Army Commendation Medal. The Army Achievement Medal. Army Distinguished Service Cross. Killed in the line of duty. Four shots to the chest. One taken directly to the heart. Fatal shot. Died protecting his troop."

Now I could feel the color draining from my face. I felt as though I was going to heave all over her desk. A sweat broke across my brow. I tried not to panic.

"No, it's a mistake! That can't be right. He's at my house. He is *not* dead."

"Sydney, it says he died the day you met him." Cheryl could sense my panic and began speaking in a soft, calming tone. She was used to talking to frantic, grieving people. I wasn't happy to be on the receiving end of her talents at the moment.

"No, it's a mistake!" I screamed at her.

"I knew there was something wrong with this guy. He lied to you. He's a gravedigger. Taking over someone else's name so he can get all the benefits."

"But—"

"Look, Sydney, here's his picture. This is the *real* Aiden Thane." She handed me the picture.

My hand flew up to my mouth. I couldn't breathe. I felt my entire body go cold.

"See, I told you. Not the same guy."

"Cheryl ..." I could barely get her name out. My voice was high-pitched and barely audible. I started to hyperventilate.

"Sydney, what's wrong?" Now Cheryl was panicking.

"*It's him.* That *is* Aiden. I don't understand. *I don't understand!* What the fuck is happening here?" I was shaking uncontrollably. My breathing was shallow. I felt like I was in the middle of a terrible nightmare.

"What do you mean, that's him? How can that be? I—"

"Cheryl, I have to go. I have to talk to him. I have to find out what the hell is going on. How can he be dead? I made love to him this morning. I've spent every day with him." Even I could hear the anxiety attack I was having in my voice.

"Sydney, I'm sure there's an explanation. Maybe it's a mistake. I'll call right now and confirm this." Cheryl did her best to try and calm me. But there was nothing she could do. I was beyond reasoning with at the moment. All I could focus on was getting in my car and racing back home to confront Aiden.

"No, I have to go. I have to go right now! I have to talk to Aiden." I grabbed my purse and keys and started to fly out the door. I could hear Cheryl as I left.

"Sydney, don't rush off. Sydney! It's icy out and you're way too upset right now. You shouldn't drive like this! Just call him. Sydney! Wait! *Please!*" She was screaming after me.

There wasn't anything in hell that could stop me from getting back home to Aiden. *What the fuck was happening?* I had to know what was going on; I had to talk to him. I needed to see him, see that he was fine. I needed to find out why the hell he was listed as deceased. I had seen the papers. They were official. I had seen his picture and there was no doubting it was him.

I started the car and pulled out of the parking lot like a banshee charging out of hell. I flew onto the exit ramp to get onto the highway. My hands were shaking and I was still having a very hard time breathing. There had to be some explanation. *I mean, he obviously wasn't dead. He wasn't.*

I could feel my car sliding all over. I knew I was driving way too fast and the roads were ten times worse than they'd been on my trip in. I couldn't find it in me to calm myself and slow down.

I came around a turn way too fast and hit a patch of what could only have been black ice. My car began to skid up a hill. I felt the car spin and it became stuck, sliding in a straight line towards a light post. I watched in slow motion as the pole and my car neared each other. I was on a straight path to collide with it. I turned the wheel and pumped the brakes but there was nothing I could do. The car wasn't responding. I was going to crash. My life didn't flash before my eyes, as I would have expected, so I took it as a sign I was going to survive this unavoidable accident. I braced myself for anything that was about to happen.

Right when impact should have occurred, my car careened to the right and I missed the pole by mere inches. I came to an abrupt stop right before an embankment. I sat there for a moment trying to catch my breath and get a hold of myself. I could have been killed.

I noticed I was still holding onto the steering wheel. My knuckles were a pure white color. I slowly released them. I tried to slow my breathing, but I was still freaking out over what was happening with Aiden. I put my head in my hands and let the tears flow freely; hoping it would help me recover my senses.

When I finally thought I was in a better position to drive again, I carefully veered my car back onto the highway. This time, I moved much slower until I reached my exit. I pulled off and jumped onto the back roads that led to my house. I sighed in relief.

24

AIDEN

I pulled into the driveway and examined my house all the way until I had come to a complete stop. I sat there for a moment, trying to calm myself more before I entered the house and interrogated him. The lights were all on. Nothing looked out of place; it looked just like it had when I left. I stepped out of the car and steadied myself against it. I was dreading the next few moments. I knew it had to be done. Slowly, I moved towards the house, but soon my pace quickened and I was running up the walkway, trying not to slip on the ice. I threw the door open and flew into the house.

"Aiden? Aiden? Where the hell are you? Aiden?" I screamed at the top of my lungs. I heard my voice echo.

There was no reply. I ran upstairs and looked in his room first. The bed was made perfectly, military style. I could have bounced a coin off it. I peeked into the bathroom, even though there were no lights on, but he wasn't there, either. I ran to my room, hoping to find him napping from our recent activities.

Just as I turned to search downstairs, I caught something out of the corner of my eye and it made my heart beat wildly. The tray from lunch was sitting on the floor to the side of the bed. Everything was there but something was terribly wrong. My head was having a very hard time processing what I was seeing. I moved closer, almost afraid of it, rubbed my eyes, and mustered all my strength to take a good look. There were two cups of coffee but only one had been used. My sandwich had been eaten, but his sat untouched. That wasn't possible. I had seen him eat it. I had watched as he had two cups of coffee. This wasn't sitting right with me.

"What the fuck? What the fuck? Aiden? Please answer me." I said the first part under my breath, but yelled his name as loudly as I could. It wasn't very loud at all. I had no breath in my lungs.

I ran to the bathroom again, because I needed to be sure I wasn't dreaming. My fear was quickly confirmed. There sat only one toothbrush in the holder, and it was mine. None of his things were there. I started to think maybe he knew he would get caught using someone else's ID and had packed up and left while I was gone. But it didn't explain the tray of uneaten food.

I stifled a scream as it built up inside me. *No. No, they were the same person. The same.* Aiden Thane was the man in the picture Cheryl had shown me. It was *my* Aiden. I knew it was him. There was no mistaking it was him. Did he have a twin? I surely would have been able to tell. It had to be the only explanation. But it listed the name Aiden. *Had he taken on his deceased brother's identity?* I began to use this thought to make sense of it in my head. Aiden had told me he was the youngest of three brothers. He had never mentioned a twin. *What was he hiding from? But the tray of food!* My head was spinning. I couldn't completely rationalize anything that was happening.

I ran back downstairs. I stood in the middle of my living room, spinning around, looking up and calling for him.

"Aiden. *Aiden!*" I hollered and then broke down, sobbing uncontrollably. It was all I could do. There was nothing left in me. Nothing made any sense.

"Sydney." I heard his voice come softly from behind me.

Instant relief washed over me. I spun around to face him, but my heart sank as soon as I saw him. There he stood, in full dress uniform. My body went completely cold. I felt a strong chill run up my spine, and my skin broke out in goose bumps.

"Aiden. What the hell is going on? I don't understand. What the hell is going on? Tell me!" I was fraught, throwing questions at him.

"Sydney, I don't know where to begin. Please calm down. You'll understand everything shortly. I promise you. There will be no more questions, and then I can explain it all. I promise you."

"Are you real? Are you Aiden Thane? Are you?" I threw the accusation at him, daring him to respond.

He nodded his head solemnly.

"How? How can that be? I saw your deceased file. I saw it. I held it in my hands. I saw it!" I was hysterical. My words came out as frantic shrieks.

I heard muffled words and then someone putting a key in my door. Aiden turned his head. I swung around and glared at the front door. It opened slowly, and Cheryl and Gina came into the house.

"Why are you two here? How did you get here so fast? I just saw you at work. How did you get from there to here with time to pick up Gina? Is this whole thing some kind of sick joke?"

But they didn't answer me. They entered my home and it was evident that Gina was crying and had been for some time.

"I can't believe this is happening. I told her not to leave. I told her she was in no shape to drive in that condition. I told her! It's my fault. I shouldn't have let her leave." Cheryl was crying, too.

"Cheryl, I'm right here. What the hell is wrong with you?" I said. She ignored me.

"I'm so sad. I thought she was finally going to find love and be happy, and now this. I can't believe she's gone." At this point, Gina turned in my direction and proceeded to walk right through me.

I gasped for air. I clutched at my chest. I felt her. I felt her move right through me! I felt her inside my very soul. My eyes grew wide, and my body went tense and cold. I felt like I was frozen. I spun around and stared at Aiden, hoping to see him as shocked as I was. But he wasn't. His expression remained exactly as it had been.

"What the hell just happened? Why can't they see or hear me?"

"Sydney, remember." His voice chilled me. I suddenly felt like I was in a fog. Images started to flash through my mind.

Meeting Aiden at the office.
The hum I felt when we touched.
Making dinner together.
Cuddled up on the couch with him watching a movie.
Kissing him.
Our picnic at the park.
Holding him after his episode in bed.
The dread of him leaving me.
The joy I felt at his return.
Finding his scars.
Making love to him over and over again.
Talking with Cheryl.
Seeing his picture and his deceased file.
Running out of the office.
The panic I felt.
Driving down the highway.
Skidding on the ice.
Seeing the light post.
And then... hitting the light post.

Everything went black. I was back standing in my living room with Aiden, Cheryl and Gina.

"I didn't miss that accident, did I?" I managed to squeak out. Aiden solemnly shook his head no.

"Am I ... I'm ... dead?"

Aiden nodded again.

"And you, you're dead as well?"

"Yes, Ma'am. I died in the line of duty almost a week ago. The day we met. The moment we met."

"I don't understand. I can't understand any of this." I was getting frantic again. "How can this be happening? This isn't real!"

"But it *is* real, very real. Well, in a sense," he told me.

"But I could feel you. Touch you. I made love to you." I was still so confused. My thoughts were foggy and twisted in my head.

"Because what we had ... *have* ... It's a gift; a gift from fate. Sydney, you and I were supposed to meet when I came home from the war. You were going to be my case manager, anyway. We were supposed to fall in love and get married, have children. But I saved all those men and lost my life. So our love wasn't to be. But fate made a deal with me, because I saved those men ... and because you and I were supposed to be together. Ours is one of those loves that is timeless. The kind everyone wishes they could find. True love. Till death do us part doesn't truly apply here."

"So you came back as a ghost to seduce me? And then to let me die with you?" I was angry with him for taking my life away. What kind of cruel game had be been playing?

"No, Sydney, it's not like that. When something changes fate, fate needs to make adjustments. Had I lived, we would have both been alive for a long, and very happy life together. But since I died, your destiny was unbalanced. Fate was going to let you die, anyway. But I begged for you. Once I was on the other side, I could feel your life force. It was calling me. Everything we were supposed to have had together. We needed to be connected; we needed to be together. So I searched you out and found you. I needed to let you fall in love with me so you wouldn't die alone. If we'd never met, even this way, we would have spent eternity looking for each other. Always missing something. Fate gave us that chance, to be together this way, in death. It's why I had such a hard time letting you leave this morning. I could feel your time getting shorter."

"So you knew I would die today?" He nodded. "And we can be together, like this?" I gestured between us.

"Forever, Sydney. Life can be whatever we want in our world. We can go through all the motions we would have in life. We could do anything. It's our choice. In death, you can be what your heart desires. That's what heaven is. I don't care how we do it, all I know is I want to be with you for eternity. Come with me."

I looked at my friends crying over my loss. I looked at the love of my life, which was truly everything I could have ever wanted in this life, anyway. He reached his hand out to mine.

I took it, and as soon as I did, every thing was right. I understood it all. It flooded over me like a huge wave crashing on the shoreline. This life we treasure was just a stepping-stone. Limbo. What was real was the love Aiden and I shared; nothing else mattered. Not materials things. Not stress. Not work. Love. Just love.

I had accepted everything that had happened. I was ready to go with him.

25

SYDNEY

I was awoken out of a very comfortable, deep sleep. It was a sudden rush of excitement and joy. It was strange how strongly you felt what the living were experiencing if you were tuned into it, here on this side.

Aiden and I had moved on to our first existence together, where we lived in a small cottage on the beach. We were married in this life, and spent our days doing whatever our hearts desired. I made him teach me to surf. There was never any fear of getting hurt, because technically, we were not in a fragile human form anymore. We were, for all intents and purposes, *ghosts*. I had been very interested to learn that I had been on the right track with my thought process on death. The soul actually was that spark of energy, as I had been convinced of in life. It just carries on for infinity.

To each other, we were as human as we had been in life. We could experience all the same senses, just enhanced. There wasn't anything we couldn't do or feel if we wanted. I know I felt love for him. It was overpowering at times. Emotions here were so raw and real. But they were only comprised of pure love. I never felt any anger or resentment. Those were egocentric emotions, only for people left in life to feel. There was never a reason to be upset here. We ate, drank, slept, took walks, and made love as often as possible. Of course there were no worries here. We never fretted over bills or things gone wrong. There was no reason to. We had it all and took full advantage of it.

I stayed connected to Gina and Cheryl the entire time. I wanted to follow the pregnancy. I would have, anyway, had I survived the accident. I still wanted to be a part of it, and so did Aiden. We watched as the baby prepared to enter the world we had just left. I guess it was an inside track. We heard every heartbeat, felt every movement, and could see how healthy the baby was. We could feel the life force. We often spent time laying on our backs, holding hands and feeling the baby together.

I turned over and reached out to wake him. "It's time, Aiden. The baby is coming today. Cheryl is freaking out and Gina is ready. Come on, Cheryl freaking out? You know you want to see that as badly as I do. There's so much joy between them. We have to go. We need to be there."

"Yes, I can feel it, too. What are we waiting for? Let's go."

He took my hand and we wished ourselves to what used to be my house. I had left Cheryl and Gina the house and my money in my will, so they could raise their child with no financial worries. They got everything.

All of my worldly possessions surrounded me here, but they no longer had any hold over me. They were just *things*. I looked around. They hadn't changed very much in terms of decor. A few pieces of my furniture were even still here.

"Look, they kept most of your pictures out. I guess they miss you a lot."

I glanced around my living room and noticed the pictures of my parents and I were still scattered throughout the room. Among them also, were now framed snapshots of Gina, Cheryl, and I. I reached out and grabbed Aiden's arm, directing his attention to a shelf in the corner. There sat his picture from his deceased file. He looked so handsome in his uniform, smiling and in the prime of life. He could still make me melt with that smile. Next to the frame sat the American flag from his coffin, in a mahogany case, and all his medals proudly displayed.

"I'm so touched they included me. How very thoughtful of them to do that. I feel like they did their best to give me a home here. I feel like family."

"They're really very sweet girls, aren't they? You *are* part of this family."

"This baby is so lucky to have been gifted them as parents. Such thoughtful, wonderful people."

Cheryl had taken a lot of time and effort in having Aiden's body recovered and delivered to her care. She had contacted his family, only to have them refuse collection of his remains. It had infuriated her. Instead, she took control, and had given him a proper military burial with full honors and a twenty-one-gun salute. She had every dignitary she could contact, anyone who meant anything that she could reach out to, attend that day. It was a full house. A few of the men from Aiden's platoon had taken the opportunity to say kind words about him. They told stories about how grateful they were for his bravery, without which they wouldn't be there to speak on his behalf.

Aiden and I had attended both of our funerals. Not because we needed to, but instead, because we wanted to. It was an unstoppable curiosity, as though we had to attend to accept our new life. I could only guess it was some sort of spiritual closure.

Gina had insisted Aiden and I be buried next to each other. We shared a plot that overlooked a garden dedicated to heroes in the military graveyard not far from the base. Our names were engraved together on one headstone, as if we had been married in that lifetime. It was a beautiful sentiment. In this existence, Aiden and I could feel each other's emotions. I knew he was truly touched, as was I.

There was suddenly a lot of commotion on the stairwell. Cheryl came flying down the stairs with suitcases in hand.

"Breathe. Breathe. Breathe," she barked up at Gina.

"Can you just relax? We have plenty of time to get to the hospital. Jesus, Cheryl, like I'm going to forget to breathe! Can't you hear me panting from all this exercise getting down there to you? This little baby is fucking huge!"

Gina emerged from behind the wall. She *was* enormous. I was slightly shocked that someone with such a tiny frame could carry such a huge weight without toppling over. She was absolutely glowing, though.

"I meant do your breathing from that stupid-ass class you made me sit through. If I had to do it, then you have to actually use it. Now breathe!" she demanded.

Gina just waved her off and took a seat on the couch.

"What the hell are you doing? Are you planning on having that baby here? I'm in no shape to deliver this baby. I'm not even sure I can get you back up on your feet."

"Oh stop it. I'm ... fine." Gina winced as she said the last part. She was obviously having a contraction. I was so excited.

"You know, they really had better hurry. That baby is ready. Can you feel it?" he said.

"I can. Anything we can do to get her moving faster?" I asked him.

"We can do this!" Aiden swiped at a picture of Gina, Cheryl and I, and knocked it onto the floor. Cheryl and Gina turned toward it.

"Look, even Sydney's telling you to get your ass to the hospital, pronto. Please don't make me beg you. We have to go. Now!" Cheryl was so cute when she panicked. It wasn't a side of her I was used to seeing often.

"Fine." Gina braced against the couch but I could tell she was going nowhere fast. "Can you give me a hand?"

Cheryl clapped. Gina shot her a death look. Cheryl helped her to her feet.

"Next time, *you're* going to carry the baby! Especially if you're going to continue to act like that."

Gina turned her back to Cheryl and headed out the front door to the car. Cheryl stood watching, with her hands up in the air and her best *what-the-hell-did-I-do* expression.

I gave her a little push on her back. She swung around to see what had touched her. We were face-to-face.

"Sydney?" She shook her head, left the house, and slammed the door behind her with a loud bang. She had been scared. I giggled at the thought of having frightened her.

We rode along with them to the hospital purely for entertainment purposes. We didn't actually require a car to get us there. But the banter back and forth between them had Aiden and me in stitches.

"I'm sorry I never got a chance to meet them in their present form. They look like they're both a blast to hang out with," he mused.

"You have no idea. I can show you a few if you'd like." He nodded. I kissed him. We found this to be one of our deeper connections, and I transferred a few choice memories of the girls over to him.

"See, that's exactly what I thought they'd be like. How lucky you had them both. Fucking hysterical."

When we reached the hospital, we split up. I stayed with Gina, whom Cheryl dumped at the Emergency Room entrance, and Aiden stayed with Cheryl while she parked the car.

Gina was being wheeled up to the delivery ward when they finally joined us.

"Are you ready, baby? This is it. We're going to be a family. I can't wait to hold that baby in my arms."

"I just want to push. Can I push now?"

"No! Just because you're in the hospital doesn't mean you can push wherever you are. Cross your legs or something."

"I want to push so badly but I' so scared right now. I just want to be done," Gina confessed.

"Oh hun, please don't be scared. Babies are born every day. Nothing is going to happen. I have a feeling we have someone watching over us. Everything's going to be okay."

The doctor and nurses came in and so began the pushing, and the cursing and the crying. And it wasn't just Gina. Labor and delivery lasted over eight hours. To Aiden and I, this was only a short blip in time.

"One more push, Gina, okay? Give me a good one. The baby is crowning. This is it," her doctor told her.

Gina pushed with all her might. Cheryl held her hand and pushed with her. They were so cute. Aiden and I held hands and watched as the small life we had been watching entered into their world.

"I give you your brand new little girl."

"It's a girl! Sydney was right. She said she could feel her. Gina, it's a girl. Look at our beautiful daughter!" Aiden and I high-fived for my winning the baby bet.

The doctor held the baby up for them to see before the nurses hurried her away to clean up and take her vitals.

Cheryl sighed with relief. She kissed Gina on her forehead. They both had tears streaming down their faces. I could feel every single emotion they did. It was amazing to know what the birth of one's child felt like.

When the nurses finally brought the baby over to them, they handed her to Gina and left all three to bond.

"Oh my God, Gina. We've waited so long to hold her. Hello, baby girl. We're your mommies."

"Do you want to say her name first?"

"No, love, you do it. You deserve to after everything you've been through to have her."

"Oh my sweet little girl. I love you so much already and I just met you. We chose to name you after someone who meant the world to us. Without her, you might not be here. Your name is Sydney. I hope you grow up to be as beautiful and amazing as she was. I just know you will."

I looked to Aiden, with my hand over my heart, and all my emotions rolled over me. Talk about being honored and touched. He smiled at me and I could feel the pride he was feeling.

"Now you tell her what her middle name is," Gina told Cheryl.

"Sydney, we wanted to honor the man who would have been your uncle, because your Aunt Nini loved him so much, and we wanted to make him part of our family, too. We know it's unusual, but your middle name is Ayden. We spelled it with a "y" so it was more girlie. So welcome to this world, Sydney Ayden Venice. I know you have two guardian angels that are watching over you. You are so lucky. I wish you could have met them."

I could tell how Aiden felt at the second honor they had given him that day. He pulled me into a hug and kissed me.

We both leaned over to look at our new "godchild" and she looked back at us. Children that young can sense our presence easily because they come from where we are. She was oblivious to everything around her, except for the four souls who gathered to form a circle of complete love around her at this moment.

A nurse entered the room, saying something about having to take the baby for some tests and that she would return her shortly. Cheryl sat on the bed and put her arm around Gina and broke into tears.

"This is the happiest day of my life, other than the day I married you. I wish that Sydney could be here with us. I'm so sorry to bring us both down, but she was like a sister to me. Fuck that, she *was* my sister."

Gina nuzzled into Cheryl's side. "I loved her, too, babe. So we'll just have to make sure that *our* Sydney knows what wonderful a person her Aunt was. We just won't let her memory ever die with her. I know she's here with us. I can feel her. Can you?"

"I've been feeling her since we came downstairs to leave for the hospital. I feel like she's been with us the entire time. I'd say it was creeping me out, but it isn't. It just feels like if I turn around, she'd be standing right there."

And I was. I put my hand on her arm and gave it a squeeze. Her head whipped around and faced exactly where I was standing.

"Sydney? Are you here with us? I can feel you. I miss you so damn much. Life isn't the same without you. It's not bad, just different. I'd do anything to see you one more time. I hated how I never got to say goodbye to you. I hated how you left me. I wish you were here right now."

"I am *always* with you. I love you. You *are* my sister, and so is Gina. We will always be close by to watch over you both and especially that baby."

"Wow, that's the strangest thing. I swear I just heard Sydney's voice in my head," Cheryl told Gina.

"I don't think it's strange. I believe she's here. I think Aiden's here, too. I can feel more than just her. What did she say?"

"She said she loved us and that she's always close by."

"I was right. Our baby has the two most wonderful guardian angels watching over her. What a blessed child she is. Thank you, Sydney and Aiden. Thank you for coming back to be here with us today."

I leaned over and kissed Gina on the cheek. Her hand flew up to where I had touched her and a tear rolled down her face.

Aiden took this as a sign to say what he needed to. He leaned between them both and whispered," Thank you for honoring me in so many ways. You didn't even know me, and you gave me more than even my real family did. I will hold you dear to me for that sweet gesture. I will watch over your daughter throughout her entire life. Now don't you worry about Sydney; I'll take care of her for eternity. Everything is perfect now. Everything is as it should be. I love all three of you."

Gina and Cheryl smiled when he finished, as if they could hear him.

"We should go now, Sydney," Aiden said.

"I know. I'm just so happy for them. It's hard to leave."

"We can stay longer if you like."

"No, let's give them some privacy. I'm ready. Can we check back in with them?"

"We made them a promise to watch over that baby, so whenever your little heart desires, we can pop back in."

"I'd like that. Are you ready to go home now?"

"Home is wherever you are, love. But yes, I'm ready."

I smiled at him and he smiled back. He put his arm around me and we moved into the light, together, to love eternally.

ACKNOWLEDGMENTS

God, thank you for everything you give to me. I know I am blessed. And I appreciate it all.

Of course I want to take this time to thank my family for their never-ending support for my never-ending endeavors. Sam and Sydney, my two beautiful daughters and my whole world, you really have no idea how much it means to know that you are there for me all the time. Girls—you are my inspiration every day!

Thanks to my mom for always being there for me and reading all my books and being my biggest fan.

Special shout out to my goddaughter/niece Chelsie Dreher—love you so much, babe.

Thank you to all my friends and family for your love and support.

I would also like to thank these GREAT military organizations: Battle Buddy, Stop Soldier Suicide, Honor and Respect our Troops, Wounded Warrior Project, One Warrior Won, Lost Heroes, Hero To Hero, and Letters of Thanks.

ABOUT THE AUTHOR

Christie A.C. Gucker lives in NJ with two daughters and a menagerie of pets. Being a mother is one of the greatest joys of her life. She has worked in the advertising industry for over 30 years as a degreed artist, but also works in the fine arts, especially sculpting out of stone or snapping photographs. Christie is also a singer and musician, and can be found singing on a few CDs.

After the death of her father, Christie searched for something to fill her desire to make a mark in this world. Her love of the arts and creativity allowed her to search for a new medium, which she found with a pen. Being an avid reader her whole life, and with her family cheering her on, she decided to take her shot, and began writing.

Fascinated by the supernatural and sharks, Christie studies both avidly. You'll be sure to find something spooky lurking somewhere in her stories. Her greatest joy is sitting on a beach with her family while surf fishing, listening to music, and living life to the fullest. Follow your dreams and never give up.

CPSIA information can be obtained
at www.ICGtesting.com
Printed in the USA
LVHW081538150722
723612LV00015B/1391